West End Boys
West End Girls

ANECDOTAL EVIDENCE

PETER.T.STONE

Order this book online at www.trafford.com
or email orders@trafford.com

Most Trafford titles are also available at major online book retailers.

© Copyright 2012 Peter.T.Stone.
Book Jacket by Ruth Edgington

All rights reserved. No part of this publication may be reproduced, stored in a retrieval system, or transmitted, in any form or by any means, electronic, mechanical, photocopying, recording, or otherwise, without the written prior permission of the author.

Any resemblance to real people mentioned in this book is purely co-incidental.

Printed in the United States of America.

ISBN: 978-1-4669-2109-2 (sc)
ISBN: 978-1-4669-2110-8 (hc)
ISBN: 978-1-4669-2115-3 (e)

Library of Congress Control Number: 2012904844

Trafford rev. 03/20/2012

 www.trafford.com

North America & international
toll-free: 1 888 232 4444 (USA & Canada)
phone: 250 383 6864 ♦ fax: 812 355 4082

Peter T Stone

BIOGRAPHY

Peter began his theatrical career as a precocious child actor in 'Oliver' in London's West End. His theatre career continued into adulthood with Rep, touring and the occasional West End credits, interspersed with appearances in film and TV. He wrote and directed for the Half Moon Youth Theatre with productions at the Edinburgh and Coventry Festivals and subsequently had a short film, 'Waterbabies of Horsey Mere' selected for the Anglia TV/First Write series. Most recently he has written and directed 'Raggle-Taggle, which premiered at the Everyman Theatre, Cheltenham and the 2010 North Devon Festival. He is a member of the 'Montpellier Writers Group'.

Contents

1. Introduction ix
2. Exit of the Dancer 1
3. Francine and her Project 3
4. The Dancer 10
5. A Producer in Paris 13
6. Lovers 26
7. Ronnie's Party 33
8. The Dancer 43
9. The Theatre Legend 45
10. The Oldest Chorus Boy 52
11. The Dancer 60
12. Hugo 62
13. Joel's Journey 69
14. For a Child Never Known 79
15. Dominic's Horizons 83
16. Old Rockers Never Die 91
17. The Dancer 96
18. A Kiss Goodbye 98
19. The dressing 104
20. Fall of the Dancer's Career 117
21. The Props Boy 120
22. Half hour Call 120
23. The Show Report 128
24. Epilogue 141
25. Anecdotal Evidences 145

INTRODUCTION

I was reading Barry Cryer's autobiography **'Pigs Can Fly'** (Published by Orion Publishing Group, 2003,) when I chanced upon a description of a production I recognised.

'You don't see acts like that now, in fact you don't see quick change acts at all, although a few years ago we went to see a magician, who did something similar. He came on dressed as an old artist with a smock and a white wig, and there was paper stretched across a frame, and on this he drew a man in a top hat and wearing tails and carrying a cane, and at that moment the paper burst open and the magician came through wearing a top hat and carrying a cane. At some point, when he was ducking behind a desk or something, somebody else had taken over the role of the artist. I love that sort of thing.'

So I wrote to Mr Cryer:

Dear Mr Cryer,

    Thank you for validating my misspent youth, for I was the 'somebody else' mentioned in your book.
    Mr Cryer kindly answered my letter and we met at my local theatre to swap stories. I love that sort of thing too!

(DEDICATION)

TO MY SON REUBEN,
I HOPE YOU HAVE THE FUN I'VE HAD.

EXIT OF
THE DANCER

2008

She is tall and slender, with small hips and a boyish cut. This is the photograph Ellen sees representing her at the time when she danced professionally. Today is her birthday. She is fifty-three and she looks at herself at the image, which depicts her at twenty-eight. She has since grown her hair. The bob has become a manageable mane and it has started to fleck with silver. At fifty-three she would expect some decay; those specks of grey on a beautiful head are the indication of her long life. She sits, looking at herself in the mirrored kitchen appliances, twenty-five years further from the picture she holds and surrounded by a collection of birthday cards. Ellen never went back to Cork, her childhood home. Growing up in Ireland, she had her family and access to a career in classical dance. She had no reason to think she would ever leave, and until she reached twenty-eight, the thought of moving away had never crossed her mind. A professional dancer knows her career is limited and when the time comes, is forced to consider retraining. This is how Ellen left her family and now it is impractical for her to consider returning. Ellen's feet are idle and her curled toes are misshapen when they are unwoven from her shoes. She no longer stands but sits, unable to raise herself from her chair. Ellen has found a new life, met a husband, had a child and then saw the perfect family descend into a messy divorce. Her child is upstairs now, thirteen years old and obsessed with his Play-station. The child does not speak with the lilting Cork accent of his mother, but rather the estuary drawl he has learned from the Camberwell district he grew up in.

The photograph she handles, arrived with one of her birthday cards, an invitation to a re-union of the production that brought Ellen to London and the postmark identifies the sender as one of her ex-colleagues. On the back of the photograph, it is dated May 1983 and Ellen's is a face amongst others in the picture. It is a section of her life, a life in a 6" x 4" framed postcard. This picture depicts the chorus of dancers outside the Regent Theatre, having a break from rehearsals and relishing their success. Ellen stands with them in the picture, happy and without the knowledge that this was her 'best of times'.

That production is now history and the company still meet yearly to compare wrinkles. She turns the card over in her fingers and breathes deeply, feeling a swell of disappointment building up inside her. It is the picture of her standing, which upsets her, those long legs and the pointed arch to her feet, alongside the youthful group, some who became winners, and some who were unlucky.

Julian, Francine

FRANCINE AND HER PROJECT

1982

Francine slips into her silks, cut high above her pubic line, revealing skin she had shaved close that morning in her cast iron bath. She enjoys the preparation before the shows, the make up and the costume. She deliberately applies her paint, delineating the face she wants to show from the face she owns. It is not the identity she was born with, for under the foundation are scars from the plastic surgery. In the accident, it was her nose that was the main point of impact. The ear has been repaired, but she is conscious of the damage. She angles her head when she meets others, thus hiding the deformity. Those in the car with her were not so fortunate. Her sister died a week later without regaining any recall, while her mother and father were killed outright. Francine survived and for the past decade she has been alone in the world.

It is seven o'clock. Within the Palais de Rouge, a small, non-exclusive club in the side streets of the Left Bank of Paris, Francine sits at her dressing table, while on stage the company have been rehearsing a new parade sequence. She has a new frock to be presented alongside the expensive scenery. In the end parade, it is the costume and her breasts that the audience will be watching with interest and she will play to that audience. Her face, however beautiful, will not appeal, for the clientele in the club are no better than voyeurs, and she is little more than meat offered to them. Although Francine is the eleventh richest woman in France, she has rejected the world of her wealth and used that wealth for other pursuits.

Since her twenty-first birthday, she has been wholly responsible for her financial situation and used her money to establish a foothold in artistic circles. The executor of her late parents' estate and her personal advisor, has been impressed by her abilities to handle great amounts of money, but has concerns over where those funds are going. She has invested in this club as well as managing estates in Paris and Mustique. Soon she will add a residence in London to her portfolio. Her guardian thinks that while property is a good investment, theatrical productions are not such a solid guarantee of return. Francine paints the final line to her face and then deftly lifts the costume onto her shoulders. The dress has been cut out to allow her breasts to fall tidily to either side of the bodice and she applies some rouge and glitter. She is wealthy and yet she chooses to work in the chorus line, in a production that is little more than a brothel with a stage.

Being orphaned at a young age was her tragedy. Her family, wealthy Parisians lived a good life, too good a life, for the expensive fast car in which they were travelling stopped all too suddenly. It took the parents and one of the girls to a premature grave and left one child to grow up rich, yet alone. Now grown up, Francine has re-invented herself as a dancer and showgirl, each night facing an audience who know nothing of her history. Her guardian, who saw the girl hold his coat tails for advice, now sees her turned into a confident woman, her place settled in an industry of her choosing and her whole life ahead of her. The press have been kept at a distance by her guardian and a discreet veil has been pulled across the behaviours of this errant heiress and her new interests, in the way only French society can maintain. If the audiences knew who was dancing for them each night, they would marvel that she could integrate so easily. She is the eleventh richest woman in France, but has no interest in her birth right.

There is a knock at the door. She has left instructions with the management that only a few select visitors are allowed to disturb her before the show. The knocks grow louder and the handle swivels, controlled by whoever feels that they have rights to her private domain. She calls in her Parisian tones to the person behind the door to wait, while she wraps a silk shawl around her shoulders to hide her modesty.

'Francine, open the door', comes the voice of the man outside.

'Wait Julian!' she finishes powdering herself and slips the key in the ancient lock to allow him to join her. He is in his early thirties and smartly dressed in a garish suit that matches his luminescent glasses. Julian is not her lover. As the son of her guardian, he has inveigled his way into her life, assisting her and advising her, sometimes against the wishes of his father, on matters of spending her wealth. He has a degree in French law and works, without enthusiasm, in his father's successful practice in Paris.

'We have found a theatre,' says Julian 'I think I shall visit London this week.' Francine lifts the corner of her mouth, acknowledging Julian's endeavours. Under her instruction, he has begun negotiations with London producer, Michael Leighton, to take her money and spend it on a new conceptual musical.

'Let me see the figures,' she commands. She has been waiting for this news. This is her chance to step out of the shadows and conquer the International theatres. He presents her with the documents and she scans them, quickly absorbing the basics.

Francine has plans to mount her own production and in secret has been building a project around her latest lover, Alessandro. Originally from Brazil, her new beau has travelled extensively throughout Europe trading as an illusionist. His reputation has grown since taking up a residency at the Palais de Rouge and he has become something of a phenomenon in the Parisian club scene. Skilful and eloquent in many languages, the magician can charm prince and pauper alike and then make best of friends of them all. It was this charm that attracted Francine. She studied his first performance, and after watching him defy science with his illusions, called him to her dressing room, for a personal demonstration. Their courtship was swift, as she was captivated by his performance on and off stage. Francine's financial influence over the club ensured that Alessandro had a future in her domain. Although she plays only minor roles in the show, she is a major shareholder in this club and by using her influence to nurture the young magician, has arranged for Alessandro to receive the correct publicity and attention. This was a disappointment for Julian, who had known Francine all her life sharing her interests in the Parisian theatrical underworld. With Alessandro in the picture, Julian's influence over the young heiress became marginalized and he ceased to be her confidant.

'I want to get dressed,' says Francine handing back the paperwork half read. 'Go to England. Do whenever you can, make it happen'.

Francine has spoken and Julian, knowing his place makes to leave, a little deflated that his efforts are not rewarded, beyond the formal relationship. She senses his disappointment and extends her hand to him.

'Well done Julian. We shall have a fine time in London. Please send in Alessandro.' And then she dismisses him with a wave of her hand in expectation of her lover. With Alessandro, Francine had found an artistic soul mate, her wealth becoming the means to his promotion. This young magician from the Southern Americas' had all the contradictions of his youth and culture. He was highly sexed and tempted by both men and women. He bewitched Francine and their affair quickly became her secret pleasure. They made love in the theatre, an exercise that Francine found dangerous and erotic. Alessandro included these sexual encounters with the passing trade, which she accepted. Through Francine, the Magician had found his place in the club, as well as a lover he, and his ambitions found their home. Over the months at the Palais de Rouge, Alessandro developed his performance character into an androgynous puppet that could wear costumes for seconds before morphing into another shape or gender. From his study of the gay revues, he worked the iconic personalities into his performance, miming their songs with their movements replicated perfectly. As these characters, he performed quick changes and magic illusions that were intricate and complex, stunning the large crowds in the club. For Alessandro this was not enough, regardless of his successes, he wanted to perform a flight illusion and he saw Francine as the route to this desire. He knew that there was a trick performed in a circus in South Africa and he wanted it. The act created the illusion of flight, not by wires, but free flight that could travel over an audience. The apparatus was dubbed the 'Cherry-picker', and originally invented for the gathering of small fruits off high trees. Using a pole and a counterweight and a harness an operator could lift, turn and travel, untroubled by gravity. The equipment was expensive and the operators needed training to make it work safely. It was a huge investment for a scene that would last a mere five minutes, but it was a showstopper! Most illusions work on the principle of directing the audience's mass attention on one focal point, while in the shadows anything could be happening. By cloaking the apparatus, the magician could create a void between himself and the audience that gave the illusion of unassisted levitation. Now he had his money tree Alessandro pursued his dream to acquire this illusion. Francine's wealth made this possible and the club agreed to allow the changes to be made to their stage, as long as she was footing the bill. With Francine, the money, the theatre's blessing and finally the audience reaction he was a sensation. Just as he had predicted, the magician flew across the auditorium to capture the hearts of Paris. The club benefited from the attraction for ten months, until Alessandro announced that he was bored with Paris. Francine herself was tiring of the Parisian club society and wanted to live in another city, so Julian suggested that they might all do well to try and transplant her protégé to the UK. Without a family to hold her to Paris, Francine was able to uproot and felt at liberty to leave when she saw a new horizon. Julian, keen to make the step from her unofficial P.A to International Producer, took charge of finding the theatre and negotiating contracts. With his knowledge of the law, he had his place of assistance in understanding the complexity of any contract beyond the simple words. Julian took the suggestion and made it practicable. For six months, while Alessandro and Francine developed a narrative involving all the magician's illusions, Julian contacted designers, choreographers, composers, costumiers, accountants and production teams. The concept entailed Alessandro to star as 'The magician who flies through time' and Francine would be by his side to make it possible. They intended casting with a mixture of French and English performers to recreate the essence that was the Palais de Rouge' winning formula, only larger. This trio thought that they could make theatrical history, which was a risk as French cabaret had never crossed the channel successfully and these were no seasoned producers. Alessandro dreamed of walking through London's society a celebrity, whilst Julian wanted his parents to see him spearhead a successful theatrical business. Francine? She wanted a platform for her lover and could afford to lose the odd million.

Alessandro stands framed in the doorway supplanting the previous visitor.

'You-a-asked for me?'

He is thin, unhealthily so and, dressed in the thin silk shirt and cream tights, showing every contour of his frame to Francine's eye. His hair is held back from his forehead by a make up scarf and he has applied the first foundations of white to his face. When summoned, Alessandro left his dressing room to be with her. With one eye surrounded by the base make up and the other sculpted to a finished image, he is only half ready for his audience.

'We are going to London.' Francine told him, looking herself like a painted doll, her body arching towards the boy in the doorway.

Alessandro enters the room and closes the door. She remains seated at her table and watches him in the mirror as he undresses behind her. In her partial costume, she reaches out to him, touching the open flesh and bringing him to a heightened state of pleasure, all the while holding his eyes with hers through the reflection of her mirror.

'You are-a-good,' he says pulling up the tights over his swollen body. Francine smiles at her lover, swallows and whispers. 'We shall be good in London too.'

He steps over to the doorway, opens it a little, just enough for him to slip through to the outside corridor. Once outside he turns to her and mimes a kiss to his benefactor.

THE DANCER

2008

Ellen fingers the photograph and then puts it down on the counter to make her coffee. She pulls down a box of medication, chooses the correct pill and when the kettle boils, makes her beverage and takes the dose required.

1982

An agency approached Ellen in Ireland and she signed willingly. At twenty-eight she was near the end of her ballet career. Although still able to perform at the required level, she knew she would soon be asked to leave the ballet and then have to find herself a new profession. It is the dancer's lot in life to retire at a time when most professions start getting into their stride. There was no lover to keep her in Ireland because, as the company travelled, she had never established serious roots. All Ellen's siblings had left home and her parents did not pressure her to return so she felt freer than she had ever known before. The audition in London was arranged by an agency and entailed taking the ferry across from Cork to Swansea and then a train to London. She had been to London once before to play a ballet festival, and while on tour, the company had been ushered around like a flock of swans. This time Ellen liked the freedom of travelling alone, but missed the security and companionship of the other dancers. In London, she was met by the agent's representative, together with four other girls, who were also being auditioned for this new musical show from Paris. As her training was classical, she was a little frightened of the steps she would be asked to present. When she joined the National Ballet, she was told that certain dance movements were not encouraged for the classical ballerina. Training for the classical dancer enforces a certain constraints, and drills these movements into the fabric of the muscles. The habit of movement can easily be broken when a contradictory form is introduced. She had been a talented clog dancer as a child, but this she gave up when she joined the ballet school and Ellen was aware she now had only a limited knowledge of modern choreography. Many in the ballet circle saw the commercial circuit as a step down artistically, she herself would also have thought this production demeaning a few years before but in these last useful years, she had little alternative if she wanted to keep dancing.

In London she was billeted at a hostel with the other girls, the agent having arranged the accommodation and an audition for the following day. That night the girls sat overlooking the London rooftops, behind a scaffold of flickering neon, there they smoked cigarettes on the hostel fire escape. Ellen was the eldest of the group and listened to them gossip as they discussed their aspirations. Sitting uncomfortably with her fellow dancers, she watched the young flesh before her and she sensed the gap between their youth and her closing career. Ellen had been warned of the regime in commercial productions, with eight shows a week and classes during the day to keep up her fitness, she was not expecting it to be easy money. She knew the hours would be long and the costumes sheer, but the West End Equity rate of pay would be the reward for her effort. This would be a fine finale for her as a professional dancer and give Ellen the chance to save for her retirement. The younger girls were giddy at the prospect of the West End and calculated the rates they could earn, unaware of their true prospects. At the audition the next morning Ellen showed the younger dancers what her years of ballet conditioning had given her. Her legs lifted higher, her arms were straighter and her smile stronger. She ached more afterwards, but that was the price one paid as the body aged. As was her luck, the French company wanted a dancer who could perform on pointes, and so she alone was hired.

A PRODUCER IN PARIS

1982

In the first week of March, Michael Leighton rang the small Parisian office and awoke Julian from his morning nap. Julian's hands flailed around the desk looking for the buried phone, while around him sat large piles of unattended paperwork. Deputations to the courts and agreements that stemmed from disagreements fell to the floor, in his attempt to find the receiver. He had been avoiding his tasks most of the morning and this workload had remained unopened and would haunt him later in his working day. But for now, between his daydreams and the good lunch ahead, Julian was glad of the interruption. At the other end of the line, Michael Leighton was the Producer that Julian hoped to entice onto the English side of this project. After the usual pleasantries, where Julian had to endure the formalities of their respective weather reports, Michael pursued the reason for the call. Julian confidently assured the London Producer that the French company he represented, had serious intent to court the Leighton's, as partners.

From his office in London, Michael Leighton replaced the receiver and considered the prospects of this venture. He wanted to believe that this Parisian businessman was a genuine envoy from a genuine source of wealth. Michael Leighton, of the Leighton Theatre Group, had an empty theatre that needed a production to make it profitable and this French project would be a viable way to that theatre's profitability.

Back in the Parisian office, Julian folded up the files in front of him, signed a few of the important details left by his father and went to his lunch. At his favourite restaurant Julian ordered an expensive bottle of wine to go with his Moules-et-frites and celebrated his step closer to a career change. Michael, on the other hand did not celebrate, his lunch plans were more thoughtful, consisting of a take away sandwich brought back to his office by his secretary. The more Michael thought about partnering with this unknown producer, the more his lunch disagreed with him. He was aware that every decision he made could have a catastrophic consequence to the family business. The family had an influence over his professional life and it was under the Leighton name that he lived and worked. Michael ruminated about this French producer, trying to picture the person with whom he had been speaking. He chewed languidly on the sandwich, as the clock ticked through the hour. Wrapping the remains of his food in a serviette, he called for his secretary to try again to make contact with the British embassy in Paris. An old friend from his days of boarding school and now high up in the diplomatic world was researching the true profile of the mystery 'Angel'. Angels are a difficult breed of theatre backer, prone to amateurish investments and little knowledge of the industry. He would be happy to work with a known investor with the funds to finance a production, but so far in this deal he had only spoken with the go-between. No partnership could be considered without concrete evidence that there was either a production, or a serious backer in the sidelines, for Michael's family only dealt with 'legitimate partners'. To Michael, the term 'business' always referred to, as if it could be none other than the theatre. There was after all, a Leighton Theatre in Shaftsbury Avenue and four generations of actor managers, agents and producers at the helm of London's Theatre-land to add weight to their claim. This alliance, with a new foreign theatrical enterprise was going to be a gamble for the family name and as a theatre producer in his own right Michael was not a natural gambler.

The Leighton Empire was a conservative concern and its main income was financed by a successful thriller running at the family owned theatre for the past 40 years. Any new production would have to enhance the company's portfolio and not eat into the steady profits of an existing golden goose. The family had trusted Michael to provide stability in the family firm and so far, he had not strayed from this course. Within the industry, Michael's theatrical reputation was built on his lack of innovation, for as a producer he had not been ready to make his own mark on the West End. He did not feel confident to fly on his own and would not commit the Leighton name to anything other than the theatre his father and uncles would have themselves commissioned. Michaels own enquiries to assess both Julian and his client, found only a well-connected solicitor with a mystery client. Eventually Michael's mole in the Embassy had been able to discover the identity of the mystery backer and some of her potted history, much of which was gleaned from the unpublished society gossips of the French newspapers. These investigations revealed a buried lineage of untold wealth and eccentricity that Michael realised he could mine and his confidence rose a little with this knowledge.

Francine's guardian and Lawyer had overseen her growth over many years and were still, even though she was now legally old enough to manage her own affairs, commissioned to promote her interests. Julian had taken more than a professional interest in this client of his father and attached himself to her social and artistic experiments. Julian conducted this attachment in secret, spending his spare hours at Francine's' side and attending to her whims. Despite the warnings from her guardian, Julian continued to encourage her in the squandering of her personal wealth in fanciful experiments. She tolerated the son of her guardian, trusting in his discretion and honesty and used him to her best advantage. The guardian had for a decade, watched over the heiress with a cool yet, fatherly hand and his dispassionate handling of her family's wealth had made her an even stronger fortune than she had inherited. It was the fortune she was now able to spend as she wished in the knowledge that there was an in-exhaustible supply. Julian, while aware of the depth of that wealth, hoped that with Francine's backing, he might be able to further his own desire to enter the world of entertainment. Although he qualified himself in legal matters, his own passions lay in the bohemian world around the French Capital and his own legal studies had suffered due to nights spent carousing when he should have been facing facts. While his Parents allowed him his youthful pursuits, they hoped he would curtail his interests in the bohemian lifestyle when he entered the family law firm. Unbeknown to his father, the carousing did not stop when Julian passed from the student world into the legal cloisters. Consequently he had not progressed professionally further in the law and found himself dulled into a submissive position in the family firm. Through his alliance with Francine, Julian courted the possibility of accompanying the young heiress on her journey of self-discovery and escaping the legal world. The relationship with Francine did not include an intimate opportunity even though this was a hope that her guardian had secretly wished for. Francine had been clear from the start that she and Julian would always have a platonic friendship, as she had grown up knowing the young man since their childhood, and theirs was a familiarity that was more akin to brother and sister. In the deepest recess of his sub-conscious Julian dreamt of a union with her, but he was the public face of this venture and he knew his part, and played it correctly.

After two months of letters and phone calls, where each side tried to weigh up the other party, Julian suggested a first meeting in London. Julian promised Michael a lunch, itself an incentive to any Producer considering a future working relationship. Within the week arrangements had been made and Julian and settled back into an airline seat heading for London's Heathrow airport. He had not spoken with his Father about his visit to London, for he kept his council well, both in the courtroom and at home.

At the Criterion grill, in the heart of Piccadilly, a few yards from the Regent Theatre, Michael, always early for any meeting, was sitting at his usual table waiting to order a luncheon and the arrival of his guest from Paris. His choice of venue and lunch was a formality for he ate here often, a favourite among the many eateries in the area. Michael wore a formal suit. He always wore a formal suit and apart from the occasional weekend, when he wore a less formal suit, he was best attired in three pieces of cloth, rather than casual wear. At thirty-five he had the figure of his father that showed his abhorrence of exercise and love of good nourishment, while he retained a youthful freshness in his face.

A young man appeared at the foot of Michael's table dressed, as if he was about to take a seat in a sports commentator box. Without looking up from the menu, Michael reeled off a selection from the card handing back the menu with a flourish. Julian stood his ground and coughed loudly to reveal he was not the waiter, but the host. They greeted each other and shook hands, sizing up each other by the grip and the small movement of their grasp. Michael was prone to make a judgment about someone's character within the first few seconds of meeting and thought Julian, a little 'flashy' to be conducting such business. Julian in turn saw an over fed English prig and was not hopeful that he would be able, or want to make a convincing pitch to this pampered bourgeois.

As introductory meetings go, this was not the textbook way of securing 'entente cordiale'. They formally made their acquaintance and eyed each other before the duel began. Knives in hand, they buttered their rolls and chose their meals. Within the first half hour and into a second bottle of Claret, Michael had warmed a little more to the young Frenchman. He did not approve of the continental dress sense, as it did not seem appropriate to the Victorian interior of the Criterion Grill. With the wine and the genuine enthusiasm displayed by the Frenchman, Michael decided to give him the benefit concluding the look was 'not all that make'th the man'. He ate and he listened to the presentation, occasionally politely interjecting to enquire about specifics of the promised extravaganza. When Julian produced an artists' interpretation of the settings and costumes already in place at the club in Paris, Michael showed a little more interest, as the designs were in his estimation, very effective. He raised an eyebrow at the mention of this 'Palais de Rouge' venue. Undeterred, Julian quickly produced a map of Paris and in a swift swish, circled the area with a marker pen. Michael peered over his glass and made a mental note of the location. They talked as they ate and Julian made no effort to provoke Michael into speaking anything but his mother tongue. Michael could manage a spluttering conversation in school boy French, but Julian dominated the table with his immaculate command of the English language.

'What does it do, this production of yours'? asked Michael.

'Do'? repeated the young Frenchman. 'It entertains'!

This answer was universal to both sides of the channel, for all a performance can be expected to do is contain a mob of people. However important the theatrical message, if it is not entertaining, the potential audience will take its collective monies elsewhere. Michael's business was a full theatre and profitability was built on numbers of seats sold. Any of Michael's negative judgement dissipated after the first two bottles of wine left the table. Each man forgot their preconceptions under the influence of good wine as they headed for the main course.

'It is a show of variety. You have variety shows in England, no?'

Michael listened to the deputation and found himself nodding and warming to the argument.

'We have a different expectation in our Variety, Monsieur Julian. Ours caters for a family audience; 'nothing that upsets the ladies and scares the horses,' is our guideline. Variety is still much alive in the Palladium and it is an entertainment for all.'

Julian did not understand what horses had to with the world of theatrical variety, but nodded as if he comprehended the remark. Julian's vision of the European style of variety included explicitly sexual activities, not a sordid erotica, but an entertainment aimed at an audience of tolerantly interested adults. French review disclosed themes which, although universal are not always presented in full frontal honesty to the English public. To Michael, the English meaning of 'Variety' was an Anglo-American fare that London audiences could tolerate. It fitted the early evening family schedules and recruited known and safe television stars as hosts. I He was conscious that the Europeans saw the unclothed human form on prime time television, but in the UK 'Nipples' were definitely not on show. Michael was not unaware of the revenue that could be made from the sex industry and knew of London's sexual sub culture. It sat awkwardly in-between the lanes around the north of Shaftsbury Avenue. One could hardly fail to see at the edge of 'Theatre land' the many neon signed entrances highlighting illicit voyeurism, which had been available for years. It was mixture of sex, alcohol and adult entertainment, and held in check by the strict Westminster Council. Every schoolboy knew of the existence of Soho where for a price, anyone appearing to be over the age of eighteen could receive a watered down drink, a paper tissue and visual stimulation. Michael himself was partial to the visual stimulus of video and had amassed a large collection of erotica that he purchased through a mail order firm, and shared with no one. He had no intention of joining the producers of this material, but he understood there was a market. Clubs in Soho earned a different type of producer a healthy living based around the unhealthy pursuits of prostitution and excess, theatre managers and pornographers were not natural allies. Michael was not sure that London was ready for this concept, but let Julian continue with his presentation, while he continued to enjoy the Dover Sole. At the end of the pitch Michael waved the fish remains away and called for the pudding. The sweet trolley interjected the meeting and they both made a selection before continuing their views.

'I never find sex entertaining,' said Michael between slurps.

'This is not sex, answered Julian quickly, 'this is the visual expression of loving.'

Michael's own understanding of the 'visual loving' was mainly a single one spurned on by his collection of fantasy lovers. What Michael had never known, and was prepared to acknowledge, to himself was that he had never been infected by the experience of love. While themes of emotional intensity are the stock of literary narrative, Michael had never been able to feel that intensity. There could have been many sexual escapades for a successful theatre producer, as his wealth and position makes a producer attractive to those with theatrical ambitions. Yet something in their look, voice, or scent would halt Michael before he undid one of his own buttons. There was a market for an erotic theatrical experience and a number of productions had seen nudity and mock fornication played out graphically for the West End audiences, but these were not the productions the Leighton Empire plc, were known to endorse. Michael did not wish to front a production with this subject matter, or see it on the family billboards. Julian argued that for the French audiences, entertainment was entertainment and if its subject matter was overtly sexual there was no reason to hide it from the wider audiences. He felt that amongst the higher art forms, there should also be a production that would give adults a safe sexual pacifier.

Coffee followed with a Cognac brandy and the differences of opinion were soon shelved, peace always reigns after a good meal. They finished their lunch and Michael walked Julian up through Piccadilly Circus towards Denman Street to show the Frenchman the Regent theatre. Although he was less than convinced that Julian's production was a suitable horse to back, he felt obliged, after all this time and energy to make the gesture of presenting his theatre in payment for the lunch. The majesty of the 1920's façade impressed the Frenchman, as they stood at the corner of Denman Street and admired the building.

'Why England?" asked Michael raising his voice to account for the hubbub of London's traffic.

'It is my Client's wish. She has a wish to spend some time in England. She also has wishes to spend her money here also.'

Michael led Julian into the foyer marching past the box office with an air of authority, for which his family name entitled him. They passed through a red curtain into the inner sanctum of the auditorium and stood in the shadows to take in the majesty of a West End space. On the stage there was a small box set representing the interior of a Victorian house, nestled between the expanses of the decorated proscenium arch. Two technicians strode across the stage, absorbed in their routine tasks and unware that they were being watched. One pushed a broom and swept the dust into a pile while the other dipped his mop into a bucket that contained a steaming disinfectant and gave the stage a watery sheen. Julian and Michael remained hushed, in reverence to the cathedral interior and watched the two men working their way across the forestage preparing for the evening performance.

Michael broke the silence. 'This production closes in two weeks. We have nothing to follow, so if you are interested . . . . it could be yours from March, at the right rental, of course.'

Julian nodded and took note of the dates, aware that Francine and Alessandro would not be free from their present commitments until the late spring. He calculated that the theatre specifications were large enough to accommodate all of Alessandro's illusions without alteration to the stage area, or decor. He noted that only the seating would be a problem, for the traditional French revue always included a sit down meal and the present rows of seating would have to be replaced by tables. Julian also calculated he would have to find a full catering department to supply the 800 potential guests and this would be an extra outlay to the increasing budget. Julian took time to picture the theatres art nouveau interior, which he imagined complimenting the colours and costumes of the Parisian club. He eyed the painted nudes embossed in the panels on the walls and wondered why the English found the moving human form more illicit than the stationary sculpture. Michael waited while Julian took his moment of thought and then suggested that they look further around the building. They toured the technical areas and then progressed to Michael's office, a palace of wood, leather and flocked wallpaper. On arriving at the theatres inner chamber, Michael broke out a bottle of whiskey from the drinks cabinet. He was not convinced that this young producer represented a viable prospect, but felt part of his method of entertaining a guest was to provide a glass of his favourite malt. It had after all, been a free lunch and he felt obliged to offer the Frenchman a traditional taste of 'English' spirit. Two glasses were decanted and Michael took a sip and started his interrogation.

'You work with your family? Julian sipped the liquor like a child being inducted to the adult world. Michael continued.

'I too have family responsibilities, all this was my grandfathers, and I am the third generation Leighton sitting in this chair if I remember correctly its a bit of a blur . . . these family trees.' Michael was skirting around to the subject of Francine and Julian, although younger than the Englishman, Julian was no fool. He knew that Michael wanted to know more about Francine, but loyalty held him back from revealing his employer and replayed his own personal history.

'I have worked for my fathers practise since leaving the University, there I studied Law and after completing what you would call articles, I now handle a selection of the clients. We have a mixed clientele, I manage Testaments, Wills and a few legal cases, but mainly I enjoy setting up new enterprises, such as this one.'

Michael poured another drink, offering Julian a similar measure, which Julian declined as he continued with his pitch.

'I have a particular interest in the arts, it would have been my first choice of career except the expectations of family are . . . well I did qualify. It was because of this interest that I have found myself looking towards London with this opportunity . . . . '

'With Madam Boulson?' suggested Michael.

'Mademoiselle Boulson has been a client of my family for most of her life and I have had the honour of being her friend, as well as business advisor. It is through her wishes that I have been making these investigations.'

Michael stopped the glass before it reached his lips and took the baton.

'I have made some enquiries of my own Julian, Mademoiselle Boulson is a wealthy and rather unconventional I believe. She is apt to invest her money in the arts and other less public enterprises.' She . . . . '

' . . . Owns the Palais de Rouge Nightclub' replied Julian quickly 'Yes. I was engaged to make the purchase, which has proved to be a rather good investment for her.'

'You will not be dealing with the day to day running of the Production then?' asked Michael.

Julian let down his guard revealing to the Englishman, his personal intentions. 'I will be leaving my business in Paris for the show's run. It has been a dream of mine to be more involved with the entertainment world and with Francine's, Mademoiselle Boulsons encouragement, it is now possible'.

'You are lucky to be able to walk away from your family's business commitments Julian,' said the theatre owner 'I have often wanted to take a sabbatical and make my own path myself.'

Julian sensed a kindred spirit, seeing Michael also shackled to a family business and expectations. After his indiscretion in speaking his own thoughts out loud, he once again became the man of law and from his inside his jacket pocket took out a document and handed it to Michael.

'This is the confirmation of funds for the production, together with an itemization of costing for the staff and the venue. I have the authority to tell you that there would be adequate reserve to both fund and promote this enterprise for a minimum of six months.'

Julian let Michael peruse the legal papers, whilst he visualised the Palais de Rouge scenery nestling on the Regent Theatre stage and Francine naked to the waist stepping from her plinth and bowing to an appreciative and full auditorium. Michael read the proposal and was impressed at the level of the detail in the budget. It occurred to him that if these unknown French producers were serious about their search for a theatre, they might be applying elsewhere to his competitors. Michael began fishing for information to see whether Julian was viewing other venues and other partnerships.

'You are very sure that this is the theatre for you? We might be a viable option as a partner, but for the right opportunity, other theatres can quickly become available.'

'I like it here' said Julian confidently 'this is the space.'

To Michael the confidence of this statement could be read two ways, either Julian was a determined purchaser, or he was naïve, he could not work out which. Julian did not want to appear to be committing to the one theatre, knowing it could compromise the bid, if he had no other option.

'Another theatre has been approached,' said the Frenchman 'although as yet we have not progressed to the same level in our negotiations . . . . Alas have a plane to catch and I need to report to my employer.' He got up from his seat and placing his empty glass on Michael's desk, The Frenchman took his leave. They parted company outside the theatre and Michael watched Julian disappear down Regent Street in a black cab, before heading back to his office to make more enquiries into the feasibility of this union. He pictured the young Frenchman in his Sports jacket and fluorescent glasses, and was a little envious of him for living his dream, something that Michael had yet to do for himself. For Michael, as a businessman the potential success of this project was limited by many obstacles. In a quick reckoning of the odds, he thought that this show was never going to happen and if it did. 'It would never be on my shift!'

LOVERS

1983

Coffee arrived in polystyrene cups from the café next to the theatre. It was the first production meeting on the first day of the eight weeks rehearsal period and Michael Leighton, the theatre owner and producing partner, wanted to be there to introduce everyone in the production team. The performers, who had been engaged were not present, the chorus dancers were having their introduction to each other at the, Urdang Dance Studios and Alessandro was rehearsing in the bar area, having insisted that he needed to spend the first week alone to prepare his props. This production meeting was to introduce all the technical departments, to ensure they were planning the same production. Francine and Julian were present and sat quietly with their team of designers, opposing them were the English fabricators and technicians ready for the battle ahead. Builders had taken over the auditorium and started removing the fixed seating and replacing the plush, yet worn flip seats with tables and movable chairs. The transformation from theatre to theatre-restaurant had begun in earnest. All the building changes were upsetting to the purists, who saw the theatre as a hallowed place of performance. It was an unusual step for a production to alter the interior so radically. The Regent, as with many other West End houses had not altered its auditorium in the sixty years it stood. All theatre exteriors change a little with each visiting production, advertisements, posters and quotations of the press are plastered across the stone frontage, however the theatre underneath remains the same. The auditorium, once constructed is left as it was designed as it is a portal to a performance and not part of the setting. The changes that the French producers had requested called for the theatre to be a whole performance space and dinning room. Michael Leighton had written into the contract that when the production leaves, the theatre building is to be returned to its former glory at the French producer's expense. This covered his theatre from any change of permanent usage and was necessary to prevent upset to the theatre conservationists.

While the production meeting was beginning its cordial welcomes, onstage the sets were being un-crated and their ability to fit into the stage space assessed by the stage crew. In the front of house, what was the extensive cloakroom was becoming converted into a kitchen and where the à la Carte food, cooked locally, would be shipped in and micro-waved. In every part of the theatre there was activity and Michael Leighton sat in the production meeting, knowing he was now responsible to the Leighton Empire plc for the production smooth integration. As a producer, Michael Leighton had cut the best deal of his working life, for he has brought the tatty interior of the theatre a much needed facelift and saved the original interior for a well needed reconditioning. Michael took notes and made sure that all the departments were singing from the same hymnbook. He introduced the proceedings and everyone in turn introduced him or herself. An update was issued describing the revised cast list, which included a selection of new costume requirements and the need for additional dressing rooms. The cast was now nearing thirty-strong and the show was expanding beyond the original brief and would grow further. Alessandro's dresser, Anita, sat quietly taking notes of the proposed running order. Anita's job was to work directly for Alessandro, making his new costumes and repairing those, which he and his assistants would be wearing for the show. Anita looked across the room assessing the technical support and was attracted to one face.

The Assistant Stage Manager or 'The props boy', as he became known, was nineteen years old and had been in the profession in various guises, for most of his childhood and all that passed for his adult life. He had been a teenage actor and then, when he could no longer appear in junior roles, ventured into the technical management because he had little qualification for anything else. The boy sat opposite the dresser and appeared to be taking notes, Pencil in hand he was drawing a sketch of Anita, the person who he would later ask to share his bed. Although the prop boy and his intended lover were in two different departments, they were destined to meet. Alessandro's performance relied on an assistant to make the illusions work. In the substitution of belief, it was often a magician's double whose actions created the artifice of magic. Alessandro had seen the boy in the theatre and approached Michael Leighton with the request that the 'props boy', be relieved of some of his other duties and become the magicians' assistant. Because the boy was to be the magician's double, he would be requiring a costume, an exact copy of Alessandro's. Anita now had two costumes to cut from the same pattern and she also had an excuse to interact with the boy. Although she was legally still married and ten years the boy's senior, she found herself lusting for the youth. His attraction to her was mirrored and both found themselves as equally distracted. In a moment of opportunity, the youth asked the costumier out, in the hope of cementing his desire. He asked her three times more, until she relented and they spent an hour in patisserie in Old Compton Street, eating teacakes and drinking Earl Grey tea. This became their courtship for three weeks and with many tea sessions away from the glare of the theatre, she learned a little about him, and he a little less about her. When they first kissed it was unplanned and his clumsy first move, the first step that led to a later love. After three weeks, they spent a first night in her flat in Holland Park, remaining fully dressed until the morning, when she rewarded him for his patience.

There are difficulties working with a lover. Anita felt that as the older party she had to set the ground rules, which were that they would not advertise themselves as lovers in work place and when at work, behave as they would with anyone else in company.

'What if I want to touch you?' said the boy, when his lips were pressed close against her ear. At that moment she would have relented, but she held firm, swinging round to face him and explained that, 'If things don't work out between us, we still need to work with each other.'

The boy did not understand her for he could only see their relationship successfully and left her bed, dressed angrily and stormed out of the flat. He walked around the streets of Holland Park, watching the neon of the all-night chemist flicker, before returning to her naked warmth, to apologise and accept her caution. From there on, the relationship had an easy momentum. Each day they shared tasks and Alessandro was the centre of these tasks. They spent some nights together, but often would go home to their separate places, he south of the river in Balham and she in the more affluent West London. The boy only broke their rules once, when he left a note, pinned to one of the costumes. She was secretly thrilled that he could not contain his feelings and she rewarded him again.

'We should go away' said Anita, not far, just a night.'

They both felt that the production contained their love and that outside their limit, that bubble needed testing. Was it London that held them together, or it was love? He suggested Brighton, 'we could walk on the beach. Shop in the Lanes.' He painted the picture and she joined him in that picture.

During the technical week leading up to the opening of the previews, both Anita and her props boy arranged to break from the building for one weekend. The boy borrowed a car from his brother, a beaten old Hillman Imp that would now be considered a classic, but at the time was little more than rolling scrap metal. On the Friday, the boy drove the car to work and parked in the street near the theatre and after the rehearsals they left for their adventure by the sea. Brighton is only 55 miles from London, but on a Friday and a slow two-hour drive, as everyone has the same idea during hot weekend evenings. On the journey, the couple uncoiled a little as each mile passed behind them. At Brighton, they booked in to an expensive hotel, just behind the seafront. He signed the register, while she said nothing. Anita was a little embarrassed at being his coupled with the boy, noticing the response from the concierge who mocked her with his supercilious eyes. The boy was oblivious and they signed in as husband and wife. He handed over cash, all his wages for the week and with receipt in hand they headed to the small room overlooking the car park and the kitchens. As soon as their boudoir was locked to the outside and before they unpacked, Anita gave herself to him quickly. Later that night she would teach him to stop and feel the senses that he was missing in his hurry to peak, but first, she just wanted him. In the morning they ate a shared breakfast then walked along the beach holding hands. Each wanted to tell the other that they were in love. They stopped under the pier and he blurted out his devotion for her, dropping to his knees and shaking with fear that she might not want him. She said that she loved him also and they cried, happy that in this life they had both found their mate. There and then she wanted to tell him, but she wanted to be in love more and held back speaking her truth. They lay together in the soft bed. He asked about her wish for a family apologising for not offering to be responsible with contraception, she said it would not matter. He had been hoping that this lover would have resulted in a child, for he wanted their love to expand into a wider future.

'But a child will not happen,' she said, 'it can never happen, I will never be pregnant.' She wanted to tell him, but she kept quiet and they slept until the morning.

They woke on the Sunday and had to book out by ten, urged to leave by the Portuguese chambermaid who was cleaning each room in turn. Outside the hotel they loaded the car with their bags and the boy turned to his lover.

'We should tell someone,' he said, 'I want to tell everyone that I am in Love!'

Even Anita's cautions flew away in the early morning sea winds and she agreed. They called at the home of the show's musical director, who was hosting a cast gathering. It was a full lunch party, with many faces from the production also escaping London. For the first time they were introduced to others in the production as a couple, rather than colleagues.

They drank wine, and like guests at their own wedding, loved the freedom of expressing their love. For three hours they held each other, the musical director played the piano and they all sang show tunes until the evening, when they got into their little Hillman and headed back to London.

'We'll still be careful?' she said.'

'"I don't want to break it, we can be careful,' he answered 'and I love you, so it won't break.'

They were on that cloud, loved-up and full of the chemical that gives the brain a sense of pleasure. She wanted to tell him, so much did she need him to know. Then they crashed in Tooting High Street. Not a serious dent was made to either vehicle and quickly each driver went on with their respective journeys. The brakes were always a little lacking on the Hillman and the boy was not the most attentive of drivers. His first fear was that he had injured his lover and hers, that he would be castigated by the brother who loaned them the car. She wanted to tell him then, but this was not the time.

When they returned the car, the boy's older brother did not mind the damage and said later that he liked the new woman. They finally arrived at her flat in Holland Park, went to her room and in the darkness she told him that she had once been a boy.

RONNIE'S PARTY

1983

We are eager to look into a home and study the décor with the curiosity of a detective, assembling a picture of the owner. In the observation we select the gender, character and comment on the morals, without seeing anything but their small amount of property. We are thieves of information, and spies against a target who have no knowledge of our intrusion. In this flat everything has its place, for everything is meticulously positioned. Shelves that house collections of porcelain, figures of beauty, tat and erotic figures are all lovingly displayed. Books line the walls in purpose built cases and ornate fireplaces have been restored in keeping with the design of this Victorian property. There are a few pictures in ornate frames, a signed Hockney print and a single wall of gilt framed theatre posters that would not be out of place in the Vatican. On every poster is one printed name in common, 'Ronnie Marks.' Rows of 'Gramophone Weekly and Record Review' nestle in alphabetical order, some collected in this decade, but most date from the previous thirty years. Scores in miniature and full size epic drafts take pride of place, his pencil markings showing their use, and on shelving from floor to ceiling hundreds of record albums. Within this room are 20 years of adult possession and 40 years of musical accumulation. The room is on the first floor and the bay window is the money view. On most days one can see clearly the foam crashing on the breakwaters and in the summer direct views of the beach add value to this residence.

Stepping back from the window, the baby grand piano sits in pride of place the lid lifted forty-five degrees for the best aural displacement while a row of expectant teeth await the polish of fingers to awaken its voice. The piano is out of the direct sunlight and the framed Degree certificate from the 'Trinity Music College' is hung above it. Beneath the piano is a thick cream pile carpet over-which ornate Chinese rugs wend a pathway to the kitchen, bathroom, bedroom and hall. Extra chairs have been laid out between the chaise loungue, occasional tables and ashtrays for the guests who are due for an early lunch. Even at this hour, the windows of the bay have been opened to allow the warming morning air to circulate. From the outside a Christian bell calls the faithful to the parish church, the chimes mixing with the birdsong and distant traffic. Inside the flat can be heard the sound of a food blender, fruits whirring into a pulp, perfect disintegration of goodness blended into a cocktail. The hands that clasp the blender are large enough to span the ten notes of the keyboard. The machine stops and a bottle of Vodka, is added to complete the mixture, a blend of memory loss disguised in the pureed fruits. The hands belong to the owner of the piano whose apartment and whose reputation will be enhanced by the gathering that he plans to hold. The kitchen table is laid out with a selection of nibbles, salads that are virtuous and appealing, dips and locally sourced breads, cheeses and olives from one of Brighton's many Italian delicatessens, all nestling in colourful bowls and covered by virgin cling film. It is Brighton at its best, home to Ronnie Marks, musical director and committed friend to the youthful Dorothy.

Ronnie has been working all through the previous night to make it 'just so'. With a glass of sweet white Riesling in his free hand, he admires his handiwork. Looking up he sees his reflection in the silver polished surface of the fridge, looks at the body he inhabits and wonders where the thin person he once was has gone. All he sees in that reflection is a large older man in his underclothes and a silk Chinese wrap, a gift from a lover long since passed. He drinks the last from his glass and heads towards the bathroom and to his shower. It is as he undress's, does one see the enormity of the man. The robe holds much in check and when released so does he. De-clothed, Ronnie stands facing the jet of water, his round undulating form, moving moments after he shifts the weight around the cascade. From behind the nylon curtain his Hitchcock shape shadows a little modesty from the bathroom mirror. In the shower he can close his eyes and just experience the water on his senses and forget. Water feeds him, a garden of flesh, stimulating all the millions of sensors that link the skin mass to his brain. Then it has to stop, for he has a party to create and guests soon to arrive.

He climbs out of his shower, dripping into a big white fluffy towel that covers most of his torso and he rubs, rubbing the cellulite and fat from his bones and achieving a dryness that would later in the day be dampened by his own natural sweat. Potions and powders are the necessity for any large man and on a shelf and Ronnie has many to choose from. He likes shopping for scents and offers his dampened body some scented relief before he adorns clothing. Dry and smelling feminine, through the cooling air of the open front room window, he walks naked to the bedroom where his blue suit awaits him. The blue suit hangs on the rail, recently cleaned and welcoming the first wearing of the season. It is of a light cloth and worn best in the summer months. Smart, functional and easily cleaned if one should spill anything on to it. The blue suit is also the suit that fits Ronnie's shape at present.

Until he begins the diet that will shed him five stones, this is the only suit that he can wear. The colour and line compliments his features and its shape was cut well by an expensive tailor. Over the years he has dieted, shed, put back on more, shed again and now is in the third see-saw of this routine and preparing to once again release the thin person inside of him. His sense of well-being corresponds to these fluxes in his shape, yet it does not affect his music, which is his constant quality. When he is upset at his shape his music is at its most creative, an antithesis of the distress he feels about his size. His social life is what suffers. He has no lover at present and will not tolerate being seen in an intimate situation by anyone while he is oversized, aware that he himself is not attracted to anyone of generous proportions. He shuns the club scene, for he feels the sight of a twenty stone queen gyrating on the dance floor sends most men away. In the gay nightclubs Ronnie feels he is the ugly duckling, nodding to the music beat with a chin that follows each pulse a fraction later. He hates to leave alone, so now does not play the field until he can beat this outline. For Ronnie this is war with a great cost, for he still likes the food and he loves to let it pass into his interior in a quantity that is not healthy. His diets occur only through his denial and denial is not his habit. Ronnie takes the cloth down from the rail and examines the pockets and cuffs for wear. It will last another season, by which time he will be back to the size he wants. He hangs back the suit and attends to the first dressing. The preparation of supported underclothing holds back the wave of skin and fat and he covers this with a vest and shirt, whose colour compliments his eyes. In the open gully of his chest hangs his favourite piece of chain that he was given by another lover many years before. Socks and hold-ups make ready for the main event. Stepping into the trousers, he clasps the lining and slips the legs around his trunks to hide the sprouting hairs, the cool lightness of the cotton weave brushing against the follicles tenderly. He has no belt, as the girth is wedged firmly to his waist. The jacket slips over the sheer of the chemise and completes the look. All is finished with a pair of light Italian easy fit shoes, which he deftly steps into without care, 'show Time!'

The doorbell rings, early he thinks, he is a little irritated that he has preparation still to complete and he thought he was specific about the time for guests. He grabs the glass and ambles from the bedroom to the hallway. Sunday is his day for guests. The weekdays and Saturday are for work and it is only Sunday that he has open house. Ronnie has chosen to live outside London society and in doing so he has accepted that one needs to import London, if one wishes to belong to it. This Sunday he has invited everyone he knows to celebrate the end to a first Month of rehearsals of the new musical opening in London. The whole company of the new show have been invited to what will be the first social gathering. Ronnie expects many to attend and it is the best time to hold a party in a production's social calendar, for the company are hungry to network and establish their pecking order. After a few weeks into a production it becomes less important to forge friendships with colleagues, for you already have their measure. The first cast party is where the early bird always catches the worm of new meat. The doorbell rigs a second time. Ronnie, facing the hallway mirror runs a wetted finger over his eyebrow and goes for the latch on the front door.

'Ta-ra!' He opens his eyes to see his closest girl friend standing on the doorstep. Mandy is from the flat below, she greets Ronnie, his home and an imagined audience.

'Babe, how . . . early!'

She stands in full Sunday best, posing in the frame of his doorway, a bunch of flowers picked from the garden below and a bottle of wine swinging in her free hand.

'Darling, thought you might want a hand with the h'orderves?'

'Thank you Mandy, All taken care of . . . all I need help with is this disgusting sweet white, which I opened before dawn.'

'Lucky Dawn! Hope she's left some for me.'

At this she steps forward, kisses the air on either side of his wide jowls and flounces past him into the front room. She is nearing 30, it says so on her resume so it must be true. Mandy and Ronnie go back a long way both professionally and socially, although ten years her senior, Ronnie has adopted Mandy as his 'Hag' and she has accepted the honour.

'Alone?' he enquires, provocatively placing his tongue in the left hand side of his cheek, knowing that she is technically single again.

Mandy throws her flowers at Ronnie and presents him with her bottle, which he regards with the contempt that it deserves.

'You said a sweet white?'

She looks around the room nodding approvingly at the decorations, before tottering over to the bay window to take a lungful of sea air.

'That view is to die for.'

'Shame you live on the ground floor sweetie, but then you do get the garden.'

Mandy shrugs her shoulders, she does have some benefits by being on the ground floor she has a good neighbour above her who regularly throws parties. Mandy has been in Brighton two years, moving there because Ronnie advised her to escape a difficult relationship. Brighton offers a late train service from the West End and when she is working, she easily commutes home by rail. Ronnie hands her a glass. She takes a sip and winces at the acidic taste of the cheap wine. Even after years of stage training her accent still slips into her Croydon twang when she lets down her guard.

'What is this wine?'

Ronnie removes her glass and taking it to the sink he pours it out, replenishing it with the vodka punch he had been making earlier.

They had been together in a stage companionship for seven years and never once felt the itch to look elsewhere. Ever since Mandy graduated from her drama school they had been close, working together, bingeing together and on one occasion, even sharing the same man in the course of a weekend. She is his muse and he her Svengarli. She has a voice he admires and she trusts his opinion, even when she had no understanding of the outcomes of his advice.

'Who have you invited?' asks Mandy. Ronnie slips the glass into her hand and the seats himself at the piano.

'Oh no one really, Chorus, stage management, a few French people, not sure what they do . . . . oh and only Michael Leighton of the Leighton Empire Circuit, who happens to be looking to cast singers for the cabaret!'

'Get out of here! Is there anything for little old me?'

Ronnie smiles and plays the chord to the opening number of the new show. In the first four notes of 'Running Wild', Mandy processes the key, the tempo and the song and on the fifth beat, joins him in the opening refrain. The room, that corner of the Brighton seafront fills with the energy of live music. Ronnie plays the complex myriad of notes, his eyes closed, while Mandy shimmies across the room in the belief that it is the Regent theatre stage. In her dream she is long legged and tightly clasped in a silk Dior dress, singing in full voice to his accompaniment. When he finishes the final bars of the second verse, he stops and opens his eyes sees Mandy's face close to his, where she plants a kiss upon his forehead, smearing him with her neatly accented lipstick.

'I have something new.' He says reaching under the piano seat for his new manuscript, 'Sing this and we shall both be famous.'

Mandy settles on the cream sofa as Ronnie begins the opening refrain of his new composition for the French musical.

As he plays a spell is cast, and a magic beyond his usual musical palette, travels from his fingers to the warm morning air. It is a new colour of sound and Mandy leaves the comfort of the sofa to join him at the piano and sees the dots dancing across the stave. Standing at his side, she sight-reads the words and the music, hers the first voice to harness his creation, amplifying the text and Ronnie's intention. When they finish, there is a hushed reverence.

'You like it? Mandy nods unable to speak to the maestro before her. 'You can sing it for Michael Leighton, if you wish this afternoon. It will make a fine audition piece.'

'This is for the Regent show? I want it, I want no one else to have it, save it for me and I'll grow a cock for you!'

Ronnie falls off his stool with laughter and clings to Mandy as they both gasp for breath. The doorbell rings. Mandy goes to look out of the window and composing herself looks down at a boy and a girl standing at the entrance doorway, early guests to the lunchtime soirée.

'Beginners Act One!'

In the following hours more of the cast and crew arrived, forty people crammed into the front room and kitchen, their coats sprawling across Ronnie's big bedspread fornicating haplessly until being claimed by their owners. Some drank the punch, others smoked various concoctions through the big open bay window, all were letting go of the theatre tensions on this, their day off.

Michael Leighton did arrive, flanked by a mousy French woman who Ronnie had seen trying on one of the silken costumes in the rehearsal room. Standing with her was her French consort, wearing an outlandish sports jacket and plastic spectacles that he believed to be the height of fashion. In their shadow was a shy Italian boy man, who scouted for talent among the guests and only drank mineral water. Music and wine flowed and a toast to the venture was made by the English producer Michael Leighton, as if he was launching a ship onto the sea. The players begin to gel into a company and Michael took great pains to compliment the Anglo French relations and thanked Ronnie for his hospitality, to which Ronnie sitting at the piano offered to première his latest tune. Just as before, Ronnie's flying song wove an enchantment in the small space. Mandy stepped forward to the piano and sang with a passion befitting the song and her mentor. Michael Leighton did not take a breath from start to finish, shocked by the beauty of the music and immersed in the aura of the person who was singing. Her voice held him frozen and after her voice ceased, he found himself tongue-tied and standing next to her. Ronnie brought them both a cup of punch and jump-started the conversation, introducing Mandy to 'Michael Leighton, of Leighton Empire Theatres plc!'

When Mandy eventually excused herself from the attentions of the Producer, she found Ronnie and kissed him heartily on the lips.

'Mandy Darling you do know you can't possibly turn me, but thanks for trying. He seems interested in you, your voice and your other attributes.'

Mandy had found herself a rich man, the dream job and all it is thanks to Ronnie's music and introduction. 'Oh Ronnie you are a dear,' at this the punch kicked in and she made for the bathroom.

She joined the queue for the toilet and found herself desperate and waiting in line with the mousy Frenchwoman with a strange facial scar. Denny, one of the chorus dancers fidgeted with her underclothing and looked hopefully for another cigarette. She had eaten too much and as well as needing to pee, she desperately wanted to vomit the food she had stuffed into her face. She turned to Mandy and surreptitiously indicated her annoyance that they had to wait their turn for their toilet. Mandy looked at the Frenchwoman and felt superior to the girl in the line. When the bathroom came free, the Frenchwoman pushed her way into the doorway, jumping the queue and claiming priority.

'Fucking French chorus.' whispered Mandy.

Inside Francine, locked the door heard the voice and noted the speaker. Although she was paying the salaries, she knew she would never be truly welcomed in this country.

THE DANCER

2008

Ellen fingers the edge of the photograph, touching the faces with her drawn index finger, remembering the date that this image was fixed.

It was sent by Denny, one of the girls in the show. Denny is now in her forties, married and living in Surrey. Every year they organises a reunion for those in the production and Denny has set up a charitable organisation to support dancers in difficult times. Denny was the 'Swing'. She did not have any particular role, but was employed to understudy every other dancer. Denny had an inflated enthusiasm for her dance that was not matched by her ability. She still enthuses about those times and has not lost this love for her time with the production and those who shared it. She still phones regularly and they meet at the re-unions, but were never close.

Ellen had her circle of friends in Ireland, yet after her emigration to London, these friends soon were lost and she made new relationships in her new life. Many names were willing to keep in contact, but few actually did and Ellen found her world annexed quickly when she was no longer in the ballet. If one is not in the ballet then one is finished as a dancer. Old dancers can return as choreographers and ballet trainers, but they are few. In one ten year cycle the whole original company will renew and just as in a lifetime, it is the younger generation who live on. In the wings, a hundred pairs of new dance pumps are waiting to step into the silk shoes, and competition has no regard for those who age.

There is a scribbled message on the photograph announcing that Denny is pregnant again and adding to the world a new crop for the ballet schools. Her output of children has been a regular since she met her stockbroker husband. Their fairy tale match has been a successful one, she set out to meet an eligible bachelor and then marry the one most likely to succeed. It was a good choice, for he has done just that. Denny arranges these yearly gatherings to keep links to her theatrical past. Ellen imagines Denny regaling her stories to the ladies of Surrey, of 'how it was all those years ago on the chorus line', her over-plump husband basking in her reflective glory at the catch he had made. 'Who would think that fat old Terry would have married a showgirl?'

Ellen always makes an effort to get to these reunions, as it is the only time she indulges the memory on her old life, and her old colleagues.

French Ladies

THE THEATRE LEGEND

1983

Jean-Paul Reme is a name that if you ask ten Parisians, four might know of him, one might have seen his work and the rest will say their parents knew of him. He appears sometimes on late night chat shows, drunk and smoking strong cigarettes; sometimes reminiscing about the past, when there will be clips of him dancing in films from the 1950's. All his interviews are careful to skirt around the section of his life during the war, when he was a collaborator. This is a man whose age is never mentioned; it is enough that he has reached this part of the decade and is still alive. Jean-Paul has two homes, one in Paris and the other on a French Caribbean Island. He would rather remain in the sunshine, but has bills to pay and women to support. There are children, grandchildren and even great grandchildren in both France and the Caribbean, all of whom have an honoured Papa. To describe the legend that is Jean-Paul is describing a man who has remained at the top of his career through half a century.

His career started as a child in the family profession. When Paris was overrun in the 1940s, Jean-Paul was already established as a young hoofer in theatrical revues, continuing his family business in the dark times of the occupation. This dynasty had weaned the young boy to adulthood with his inherent blood impregnated with grease paint. Jean-Paul started as a dancer and quickly moved to crooning the popular songs of the day then, as the cigarettes took his voice, he became a comedian and found fame in the cinema. He was not naturally funny, but his delivery had a dry wit and he found that the audience trusted the words of his writers. He appeared in a selection of romantic comedies and became a familiar face on-screen, films that still find a place on the French late night channels. Jean-Paul Reme had a charm on the camera and a gravelly voice that recorded well. When the film roles ceased, he moved into the club world and became the master of ceremonies and a popular director of the Parisian revues this is where, in his late sixties, he still performs six nights a week. He is still well groomed and walks tall with a full head of hair and a suave scent that follows him. He has little to complain about and little to achieve.

When he was called by Julian and asked to help with the direction of the show in London his first reaction was to laugh. He told the young producer that he does not go abroad to work. He goes abroad to play. He does not speak English and has no intention of trying, so why should he want to go to England?

'The show needs your eye,' said Julian, truly desperately to get an ally in the production. 'Alessandro means well but he cannot direct.'

Jean-Paul had experience of the young magician when he was directing and compèring the Parisian show. He did not like the illusionist; for that matter he did not like, or trust Julian and he found Francine, ambitious, objectionable and unladylike. Julian presented a list of attributes that he believed the old professional could bring to the production and pleaded for his help. In London Francine and Julian were concerned with the time wasting that Alessandro was making of the rehearsals and felt the production needed the eye of a seasoned director. Promises were made to Jean-Paul that he could send over some of his favoured people, and he was welcome to include any acts that he felt would add to the project. Jean Paul had one request that he stipulated would be a deal breaker.

'I will want to produce a prehistoric scene in which Dinosaurs of the past fight with each other, then I want them to dance!'

Julian took a sharp breath, for he could not visualise Jean-Paul's vision, but he could calculate the cost. After some negotiations, a fee was agreed for Jean-Paul together with accommodation for six weeks. With an apartment in Central London for three people, his fee and travel costs all added to the spiralling costs. ' . . . and we shall need a maid,' said the Director.

When Jean-Paul arrived in London he was introduced to the company as the new 'Director', nobody had informed Alessandro that he was handing over the artistic reins and so he promptly left the theatre for the day to compose himself. The arguments between Alessandro, Francine and Julian went on well into the early hours and then beyond by telephone, but by the following morning all had been settled amicably. Jean-Paul did not change very much in the production. He had to work with what he had in front of him, a motley collection of half-baked clichés and shambles of scenes that Alessandro had developed from his ideas. Jean-Paul made notes and forwarded his suggestions. The gaps were obvious to the experienced director and he quickly solved many of the problems that he had noticed. Alessandro was forced to admit that the old man knew his business and bowed to the new director for the help. Jean-Paul spent a further week, working with the artists on individual scenes. Sitting next to the American choreographer; he would whisper his ideas through the translator to the individuals. Those he knew from France, he called across to his chair and spoke in a hushed fatherly way, to reassure them and direct them to a more polished performance. To the English performers he would hurl abuses in his coarse French dialect that would be translated into specific directions. He somehow managed to coax an acceptable performance from his company so that they would deliver a show, to which he was happy to attach his name.

In the rehearsal period, people began arriving at the stage door from Paris, acts that Jean-Paul knew worked in the 'Palais de Rouge', acts that he could be sure had worked for decades in his Parisian show. Pedro arrived with a box of tambourines and Jean-Paul incorporated a Spanish dance into the script, incorporating Alessandro tangoing across the stage swapping himself from man to woman at every other step in a clever trans-gendered costume. Two beautiful black nymphs arrived to the theatre unannounced, unable to speak English yet expecting to play a part in the production. The girls were taller than anyone in the company and the first to remove their clothes as bid by the director. He wanted them to join the chorus as clothes models, dressed to adorn many of the scenes, for they could do little else. A giant man arrived on the same flight. He was more difficult to place in the show but Jean-Paul knew him of old and liked to have his 'little theatre monster' around him while he worked. After the second week in which Jean-Paul had made his alterations, he was ready to add the 'prehistoric' scene that he had promised Julian. At great expense a set had been designed, built and delivered. The stage crew hung the backcloth in the only available space and rocks of polystyrene were placed on the floor that represented rock falls, yet looked more like shaped rocks of polystyrene.

Then two more women arrived at the front of the theatre. They did not speak, but were recognised by the French cast and welcomed as if theatrical royalty. Both women had their eyes shielded from direct sunlight and were dressed in expensive suits, advertising the ease of the Parisian to create effortless style. Jean-Paul halted rehearsals for the day and went upstairs to greet them. After the formal kisses, the group toured the theatre, inspecting the fabric of the building, the women occasionally lowering their dark glasses to observe some of Jean-Paul's additions. The two women had an audience with Alessandro to admire his costumes and with a seal of approval, touched his face tenderly. They were less polite to Francine, whom they saw as a threat and ignored her request for an audience. At the arrival of the women, Jean-Paul's manner changed, he became jovial and excited, announcing to everyone that these were his performers for the prehistoric scene. They watched as twenty technicians ran around the stage with polystyrene rocks and placed them down at the specified places marked with coloured tape. From the heights, a backcloth was flown in and the set was complete.

'You will be fantastic!' said Jean-Paul to his women. 'It will stop the show and you will be my London triumph!!' and he kissed their hands and they bowed their heads to him.

Jean-Paul had been presented with a flat in Onslow Square. It was a spacious two-bed-roomed apartment in an upmarket area, with a generous aspect and a view to the front of the private park. After approving the stage set, The Director and the two women took a taxicab back from the theatre straight to South Kensington. Jean Paul was aware that the ladies had been travelling since the early morning and wanted to freshen up. As Jean-Paul would always stop rehearsals for lunch and often not to return until the following day, he was not missed. In the taxi to their new home the ladies did not speak, preferring to observe the squalor that was the city of Westminster. All three sat looking out of the windows at different angles, watching central London pass by at street level. The women remained masked from the world by their dark glasses and distanced from their environment. They arrived outside the apartment building, leaving the driver to struggle up to the flat with all the baggage. When the door closed on the outside world, Jean-Paul asked the two women about the family, his children, Parisian gossip and then opened a bottle of champagne to celebrate their arrival. The women both removed their sunglasses; their eyes were still bright but surrounded by older skin revealing tired crow-footed faces, painted to a fine finish. The wife was older by a few years, her hand bearing the golden wedding ring she had worn for the past two decades, and her belly the wounds of two children. The mistress, no autumn chicken herself, had fewer lines and had not provided Jean-Paul with the French son he wanted.

'You like it?' he asked, his outstretched arms describing the decor.

They nodded and walked around sipping their champagne and fingering the selected ornaments with disdain.

'I will shower,' he said and walked out of the reception room towards the master bedroom, loosening his tie en route.

'Et toi?' said the wife to the Mistress, 'It's your turn.'

The mistress put down her glass and followed Jean-Paul towards the bedroom. There was a moment's silence and then the sounds of clothing being dropped, a shower door clicking open, water running and then the closing of a glass door. The wife looked around the room happy to be alone and able let down her guard. So far she had not been impressed. They had been planning to go to the Caribbean Islands for the summer and now they would have to spend these six weeks here. She put down her glass alongside her fellow and walked into the bedroom, in the en-suite the sound of running water mixed with the occasional voice. She looked at the large bed and saw the cases laid out. They would need unpacking and she did not want the hired help to finger her clothes. She undid the leather straps of one of the cases, dialled the combination numbers of the lock and unclipped the catches to reveal the expensive layers of silks above the bright coloured linens. Beneath these were the thin-laced underwear and hosiery that he liked them to wear. She dove further under the lace to a secret divider concealing a selection of toys, shackles and straps, batteries and hand cranked pumps, leather girths that could tickle and stimulate. She selected a few items of sheer clothing and placed the selection onto the bed alongside the collection of sex toys. Then the wife removed her jacket and hung it in the wardrobe. Reaching over her shoulder, she deftly unzipped her dress linking the other arm to loosen the garment and letting the silk slip to the floor. She stepped out of her clothes and placed them on another hanger and unhooked her bra, her engineered breasts staring forwards above her tanned and rippled belly. Removing her panties, she placed her undergarments in a drawer and thought the décor cheap. In her handbag she found a box of Sobrani cigarettes and her thin gold lighter, which she used to combust the thick scented tobacco. She could see herself in the mirrors as she smoked and smiled as the Russian smoke coiled around her, her image smiling back.

The shower stopped, the wife heard the sound of the cubicle door and four feet climb out to dry themselves. The wife, with the cigarette clasped in her teeth climbed into a thong of dark red leather and taking two silver pointed cups, placed them over her raised nipples. Moving the cases to the floor, she lay on the bed with her arm lifted above her head letting the smoke drift upwards to the mirrored ceiling. Above she could see her body reflected taut, yet worn.

Jean-Paul and his mistress dressed after their shower, shuffled through from to the bedroom. He was naked and aroused. His face covered by a black leather mask and was being led by a collar and chain around his neck. His mistress, wearing a black-leather Basque, struck him at every step with a flailing stick, a faceless dominatrix leading him to his wife and the expectant courtship.

Hamish

THE OLDEST CHORUS BOY

1982

Hamish Brody is the country's longest serving chorus boy. At 47 he is unlikely now to make the grade as a male lead, but he has always been able to sing a bit, dance a bit and play the character roles or understudy. He is what they call 'competent' and the industry relies on the competent and reliable.

When he received the call from his theatrical agent he did not stop to consider whether his future lay in a touring children's show, playing an otter in a production of the 'Water Babies' for a second time. He was not keen on taking this tour and hated the costume, the company and the other otters. If there were nothing else for the summer he would have to accept the contract. Hamish knows that this might well be his last season in the chorus. His joints are seizing up and he has had a recent bout of illness, and a diseased lung that led to a cancer scare. From what his agent Dolores had said, Hamish thinks that he will be too old for this show, but it will be for the company to decide. Hamish dresses younger for the audition; the greying temples are pushed behind a baseball cap, a baggy tee shirt and tight Lycra vest beneath it. It has 'Choose Life' written across the cotton front and was not his choice but that of his Dutch lover, who found it on a market stall and thought that since all the young men were wearing that sort of thing at auditions, Hamish should do likewise. Hamish is well preserved for his years and despite the marching grey hair, he could be taken for a worn out thirty year old.

He cycles everywhere, wearing cycle shorts over his muscular pert behind which Dieter thinks it is Hamish's best asset. Hamish prides himself on his physique, twice a week he is at the gym, not just to watch the other men but holding back his own fears of ageing. Dieter has, over the past fourteen years of their relationship stopped fighting the tide and let himself go, his only compromise to age being that he has changed to a vegetarian diet. Hamish pretends to his lover that he has also forgone meat but he cannot the give up the taste of flesh so easily.

This audition will be the first West End call Hamish has had this year and even if he does not get chosen, it feels good to be still in the running. Hamish enjoys a light breakfast of juice and toast without butter. Dieter does not want Hamish to eat dairy as it affects his singing. They sit together across the kitchenette table in their cramped flat and chew slowly in silence. It has been their home for the past ten years and they will probably die together in the same rented location. Hamish prefers to live close to the centre of London and cycles everywhere rather than uses the public transport. Cycling to the theatre will help him warm up for the dancing and he can practise his song as he travels. He would have had a cigarette in the old days but Dieter had banned them after the scare with his lungs. There are many things Dieter has banned Hamish from doing recently, as they age he is more of a mother than a lover.

Hamish has an old style racing cycle with panniers and silver mudguards that he keeps on the balcony of their council block.

He pre-plans the route before leaving, which is a preparation he believes will keep him safe. From Old Street, he will skirt westward down through Holborn Circus and along Shaftsbury Avenue to Denman Street only a thirty-minute journey at most. The audition will be a private interview arranged by his agent. An 'open call' is a cruel exercise, especially for dancers. It is not like the scenes from 'Fame'. The kids do not dance on taxicabs to the pulsating disco sounds, before going on to wow the employers. The open call makes the actor wait for hours before the few minutes of rejection, or a place in the chorus. Thanks to his agent, Delores this is a 'closed call', a private meeting between the performer and the directors. He will be one of the selected professionals with a presupposed reputation before him. In his panniers he keeps a folder containing his music, CV and photograph, the picture of him a decade before. Compared to the publicity image, he has weathered well, but he has weathered. When Dolores rang she said, 'Darling no dancing you'll be pleased to hear, I think they want to have someone with experience to do some mugging and I knew you could do that admirably. Oh another call, good luck darling, call me when you have been into see them,' and then she cut him off.

That was all Hamish knew apart from the venue, day and time. He knew of the musical, hailed by the trade papers as a potential smash hit in a tired London theatre scene.

12:00am

His route crosses down through Holborn past the umbrella shop and the antique booksellers, near the museums that might be his treat later. He gets a speed up if all the lights are in his favour and he loves the feeling of wind in his face, just as he did when he was riding through the Edinburgh streets of his childhood. The cycle crosses past the Palace Theatre where in his early days Hamish played in the chorus of 'Jesus Christ Superstar.' It's still running, years later with a younger group of disciples. He enjoyed that job and still keeps the programme with his name printed in bold. Along the lower Shaftsbury Avenue he passes the Queen's Theatre, Apollo and the Globe, where he was once an understudy in a Noel Coward play. He never actually went on, but still likes to say in company, 'he once played the Globe'. This private audition is set for 12:30, not the best time to be seen, as the directors will be tired of hearing the succession of wannabes singing 'summertime' and only thinking about their impending lunch. Hamish had thought about preparing a scene, but decided as this is a French musical he is going to sing, if asked, 'Plaisir d'amour'.

He reaches the theatre and locks his cycle up against the railings. As he walks up the alley to the stage door a rendition of 'Luck be-a-lady tonight' greets him from the bowels of the building. Prudie, the stage door and daytime security lady, buzzes him in and checks his name on the clipboard in front of her. Prudie is . . . actually Prudie was fifty-something sometime ago and has lived in Berwick Street for most of that half century. She is a gatekeeper to many a future career and has power over the auditions, even stronger than that of the directors, for Prudie will not let anyone pass her stage door unless she likes the look of them. She is skilled at selecting good men by sight, for she spent much of her youth as a prostitute in the surrounding Soho districts. The selection of the right punter would reward her with a 5 shilling 'quickie,' while the wrong face would leave her beaten and bleeding unsympathetically in an alley near to where she now sits. It is a job she has held for ten years with her only theatrical ambitions being that she retires in the comfort of this post.

'Downstairs dear, turn right and someone will meet you. Good luck.'

Hamish follows the directions down the tight stairwell and is met at the foot of the stairs by Jo, a round pudding of a girl in her twenties. She checks his name on her clipboard with the other hand she is holding a doughnut.

'You'll be meeting the producer and Mr Reme the director. You'll need to sing one song, speak a sentence in French, and I shall need your agent's name and number, should we need to contact you for a recall.'

This given, Hamish is ushered into the gloom while he tries to remember his greeting in broken French. In seconds he steps out on to a lit stage, empty of scenery apart from two pianos. One piano is a fake and looks half assembled, pipe work and wood pinned together chaotically. From the darkness of the auditorium a voice calls out.

'Bonjour Monsieur Brody, ç'va?'

'Très Bien?' comes the stuttered reply from Hamish, remembering his manners.

The accompanist appears from the gloom of the orchestra pit, wiping his mouth from his early lunch.

'What are we singing then Mr Brody?' Hamish hands the music to Ronnie Marks. For Ronnie it had been a rough morning. He is the Musical Director demeaned to play the role of the accompanist today and he is not enjoying it. He looks at the score and then eyes Hamish up and down, while the side of his mouth is sucked inwards.

'Oh Plaisir d'amour. How original, only the third today.'

Hamish ignores the rebuff, certain that they have not been lovers in the past. The music starts and Hamish clenches his buttocks and begins to sing the opening refrain to the huge cavernous auditorium.

He sings, making a sweet appealing sound that echoes around the empty space, stopping workers in the building who listen to the chorus boy singing for his future. After one verse the piano stops playing and a voice calls out.

'Merci, Monsieur Brody.' Then silence followed by some unintelligible whispering.

'You will please us to return this afternoon, s'il vous plait?'

'Come back at 3 pm,' said Jo linking her chubby arm into Hamish's and whisking him off stage. 'They like you.' She sounds surprised.

Hamish walks up the stairs to the sunlight and leaves the theatre, smiling at Prudie on the stage door. 3 pm. That would give him two hours to pull himself together for the recall and a second chance. Prudie recognises him as he leaves, not as the dancer, but as the man who ported her through Bart's Hospital when she had her gall bladder removed. She never forgets a face.

There is a café outside the alley in Denman Street and he walks in and orders a steak sandwich on white bread and a coffee. Dieter would not approve of either, but he is not here and Hamish feels immortal.

The taste of processed food is a reward for his success in the audition. If he was the old Hamish, he would have sat there for another two hours and smoked until the recall, but Hamish feels restless. He decides now is a good time to see his agent Dolores, as it always pays to keep her informed that he is still living. Hamish knows that Dolores is looking for new stock of actors. With the recall as a mark of his potential earning power, it could secure him representation for a little longer, for without an agent it is known that in the industry 'you were better off dead'. Delores is one of the old school agents, still working from a mews office in W1. She is honest and was once well respected. She knows everyone who matters in the industry and the industry know her name because of her years of service. Her reputation has become lessened as she herself ages and she no longer has a thriving business, like an elderly barber who loses his edge, the industry feel safer elsewhere taking their business elsewhere.

From the Regent Theatre it is not far by cycle, Hamish can easily get to her and back in time for the 3pm recall. He leaves the café and cycles up Regent Street to the Oxford Street crossing and then cuts up to the northern end of Portland Place. Outside the small mews office Hamish locks up his cycle and rings her entry phone, gaining entrance to his agent's empire. The office is full of stacked paperwork, none of which Dolores could have referenced and never filed. She sits in a cloud of smoke behind a desk, searching for something under a pile of scripts that she will never read, before assigning them to her clients. The phone hangs from her shoulders like a fur stole, draped around an Edwardian aunt. She puts down the phone and beams a greeting to Hamish.

'Darling come in, sit down, two minutes of my time of course, don't mind if I smoke? Filthy habit will kill me one day but who cares, not the industry. You didn't get it? You did, of course you did! A recall, yes that is good as well. When? Even better so they don't have time to forget you. It'll be good to have you working, there is not a great deal out there at the moment, bit quiet as they say. Oh that kids tour fell through, something to do with the funding after the reviews last year, bloody Arts Council. Well it'll be good if we can get you into show.'

Then another phone rings, under the remains of her lunch and Dolores turns her attention to one of her more successful clients. Hamish leaves the office and picks up his cycle. He joins the main stream of traffic and heads down towards Oxford Circus past the BBC at Portland Place. He never made it in radio with his voice; apparently its pitch is too high for recording. His only original asset, his Scottish accent, had been beaten out of him when he came to London to train at the Studio 68 drama school. Consequently he has always featured in movement roles, his philosophy being that the industry 'always need a good Dalek.'

Hamish jumps the lights and cuts down past the Palladium where he had once torn tickets in the front of house during a dry spell in 1976. This is where he saw Bing Crosby's last show in London. Bing was in his seventies when he played the Palladium. He too, showed the critics, who always think performers are washed up at forty. He turns the cycle down Warwick Street, right and sharp left into Brewer Street just as a Post Office van reverses out to greet his path hard!

'The three o'clock recall hasn't shown up' rang Prudie from the stage door to Jo on stage level. 'Best send the next one down,' says Jo. 'Mr Brody obviously didn't want this job enough.'

THE DANCER

2006

The ex-dancers have been meeting at the Criterion Bar, which is only a short hop from the Regent Theatre and often will visit a show together afterwards, 'for old times'. Ellen has found this past year harder than others. James, her ex, has now left the country with his new wife Eloise, to reinvent himself as a French landowner. There is less money now and, at thirteen, Jack is starting to cost her more as each year passes. He will not say so, but Ellen is sure Jack is already missing his dad. Ellen has a disability income and other benefits that are dependant on the state of her health and the government adjudication. It is not part of her grand plan to be reliant on the state handouts and she has learned to manage with what life has thrown at her. It was a shrewd move of hers to take the mortgage out in her name, it helps having the security and ultimately, she will have something to leave Jack.

She has not told James yet, as Ellen does not want him to give up his new life and come back out of pity when he was so determined to have a new life and a fresh start. For years Ellen and James had been happy. Dependant as any disabled person is, they worked as a couple, and everyone said she was fortunate to find such a man, considering her situation. Ellen and James ate together, made love, planned growing older. Jack was a lucky result and she thought this would last.

There were doubts as to how they would conceive, but they did, just the once. Ellen believes in the power of miracles and knows that in her religion, it is wrong to ask for too much. For all his failings, and there have been many recently, James has provided for them and will continue to do so, if he can. Ellen has lived nearly as long without using her legs, as she lived with full mobility. She chose not to go back to Ireland after her accident. James became another reason to stay. James was her physio at Stoke Mandeville that was when where they became lovers. This led to twenty of her happiest years, the last thirteen with her son Jack as part of their family. They set up home in Camberwell, so that James could work at the Kings College Hospital and over the years they were able to buy a small house with some of her compensation money and have it converted with a grant from the council to make it wheelchair accessible. Ellen's mother approved of her daughters husband and accepted that she never returned to Cork. London is Ellen's home now, not once has her mother thought of asking Ellen to return to Ireland.

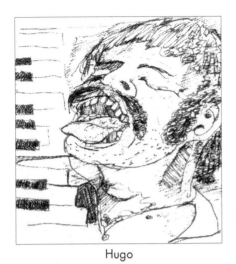

Hugo

HUGO

1983

'Yes mother I do rather love him . . . Well he's complicated, but healthy! I'm sure Daddy will like him, eventually.'

Hugo waited while his lover told her parents the good news, knowing that his introduction would be the start of a new life together in England. He could never really describe himself, as he was ashamed of what his God had given him. Only she could see his beauty and for this alone he could love her. Hugo is exceptionally tall, gigantean in fact and the moustache that adorns his upper lip is also in proportion to his size. When he meets new people, he will not look at anyone directly. He is a lumbering child of a man and as a result speaks to few, for communication is the embarrassment that is common to someone who lives in an oversized body.

Hugo arrived at the invitation of the French director who kept him employed as if he was his exotic beast. He was expecting to join the company in London as their new fool, playing similar roles as he had in the Palais de Rouge show. The director announced that Hugo would join every scene starting with the tambourine number. It was a part of the show that never worked, no one mastered the steps and Hugo's incompetence was only a mirror image of the chaos around him. Jean Paul made other opportunities for Hugo, as every circus needs its monster, this show needed him. Rather than returning him to Paris, the director insisted that Hugo remained in London and company kept him as they would a pet, a role he played to perfection. They tried him as the ringmaster in the cat scene, but he could not operate the whip. In the Venice sequence, he had to stand motionless with a torch, but his face would not remain impassive and the dancers complained that while they were struggling to keep composure, the audience were watching the oaf make fun of them all. Hugo did not realise that he was doing anything wrong. He was the true innocent, unaware that there was even an audience!

Hugo's last chance was the piano scene. The show needed a 'curtain warmer', a scene that preceded the big production number while scenery was being changed. This interlude preferably had to make a great deal of noise to hide the construction behind the curtain, and Hugo's act was perfect; as it was three minutes long and noisy. Hugo's stage act is the comic set piece of a giant sitting at a small grand piano miming to Jerry Lee Lewis. As the music begins the piano takes on a life of its own. It is a usual device in the French musicals, for artistes to mime to a recording and it is an acceptable art form on the continent. A mimed performance is still frowned upon by the discerning British audiences who believe that it detracts from real talent. But Hugo cannot sing, so he has to mime. He cannot play a real piano, so he has a trick instrument, and he finds choreographed movement difficult to remember, which means every performance is a one off. When he depresses one of the keys, the piano dances. In reality the piano moves on chambers of compressed air that raise the corner of the instrument to create the appearance of movement. Hugo is an instinctive performer he can do little else, for he is unable to predict what is going to happen when he operates the pipes. He does not care for the prop that controls him, for he is assaulted by the piano and often hurt in the process. The fake piano was shipped across from Paris and all the crew were curious about the mass of piping and wood and perplexed by its lack of instructions. Hugo tried to explain the method of assembly and eventually the crew put a version together that resembled a tuba escaping from a packing case.

'Goodness Gracious, Great Balls of Fire!'

The soundtrack to the scene was a moth eaten cassette that had been played so many times that Jerry Lee Lewis deserved a new platform.

Jo, the Deputy Stage Manager was sent to purchase another recording and took Hugo with her, making a subterfuge for the technicians to test the piano without Hugo in the building. She had been watching Hugo for the week's rehearsal and had developed irrational warmth for this odd giant. He in turn, had followed her around the building, making excuses to speak with her. His attention focussed on bright her eyes and her over shapely figure. Despite their mismatch in height and nationality, a carnal understanding was developing. As they left the theatre, Hugo gentlemanly took Jo's arm and they walked down through Regent Street to the HMV shop, his height and her girth looking a strange combination in the fashionable Capital streets. After purchasing four cassettes of the music, they sat in a coffee lounge and she asked him to tell her about his family, a subject that he had not spoken of before to a stranger.

He told her his father was from Russia, a Jew, who with other family members, escaped the ravages of the tyranny they called the people's revolution. It was thought that in the Russian revolution and the Marxist uprising was for the common man, but in reality it was for a common man that did not include the Jew. Many Jews fled south at this time in history and the family settled in France ninety miles south of Paris. As blacksmiths they were easily employable and developed a family business. After the death of Hugo's grandfather, his father inherited the business. He did not marry and had no cause to find a mate while he cared for his mother. The business prospered, as he was well respected for his abilities to smelt and weave metal. In the summer of 1940 when Hugo's father was 35 years old, the country was overrun and the population restricted by the Germanic invaders. As in Russia, the blacksmith and his sick mother were pilloried for their race and religion and eventually sent to a transit camp. Fortunately for the blacksmith, he was a valuable person to the German war machine and his skills ultimately saved him from worst slave work. His mother could not find such patronage and slipped away within weeks to join Hugo's grandfather. In the smelting works in the camp they produced ironwork for the buildings and shackles for the parties of workers who helped construct the railway outside the camp. He did as he was told and worked hard. His reward for this compliance was that he was kept alive and did not wither as many around him. In the camp, there were jewellery workers who took the gold and precious items collected and it was Hugo's father who smelted them into bars of metal for the Reich. Hugo's mother, who had been a skilled jeweller before the war also, escaped the fate of extermination, by her ability to work alongside the Blacksmith. She was 19 and he 36, yet despite the difference in their ages, when they met they were enraptured with each other. They made love discreetly avoiding discovery by the guards and in time conceived a baby. This was unusual, for there was little love making in the camps and very little fruit born by such unions.

Hugo was an odd child when he arrived. His head was disfigured and his limbs uncoiled to an extreme length, but he was loved by his parents who hid him from the authorities, long enough for him to see the arrival of the liberators. To his parents, Hugo was a miracle. The blacksmith that had never been intimate with a woman thought that he would never marry. He only ever loved his mother, his religion and his work, yet in the evil world of the camps, he preserved himself and his bride. This camp, however murderous to many, had given him a family of his own, and he thanked his God for the blessing. When the internees returned to France, they returned as a new family and this is how Hugo spent his first fifteen years. Hugo was not a clever child, but he was strong and grew to a stature that was twice that of other children. His mother was slight and his father, although strong was no giant, but families are a strange mixture and sometimes throwback to many preceding generations. Hugo joined his father at the forge until on his 16th birthday a local villager visited the family and announced that Hugo had impregnated his daughter. When Hugo was summoned to account his actions, he was seen making an exit across the fields and did not returned to the village. Jo sat back in her chair, after the narration she was winded by his revelations and disappointed that he had a child.

'Have you never gone back?' She wanted to know. She wanted to know about his child. He told her that there was no baby and the villager was only trying to stir up racial hatred in the area. Although exonerated, Hugo felt he had shamed his family and could not return to the village. He travelled to the city and joined the army, it was the year of the Algerian conflict and he found himself, a teenager, fighting the Arab guerrillas in street battles. He only returned to France after a further six years travelling, by which time his father had died and his mother had been confined to a mental institution. It was while in Paris that Jean Paul Reme, as Director of the Palais de Rouge nightclub, discovered Hugo and offered him work clowning.

And you?' he asked of Jo who sat open-mouthed listening to his life story. 'Et Toi?'

Of Jo's story there was little to tell. A normal family, also Jewish, with her life had been spent in the safe opulence of political security. This blessing of geography allowed her to grow up with a family and enjoy safety and an education.

'Shouldn't we be getting back?' She said to him, as she wiped the cappuccino froth from the hair on his top lip.

They left the coffee house and walked back, magnetically joined unaware that their hands were touching. Hugo's rehearsal should have started twenty minutes before. Jo let go of Hugo's hand as they walked up the alley to the theatre stage door. Prudie, on the day stage door was reading her magazine and released the buzzer without looking up. At stage level all were anxious to get the piano tested and the stage manager was getting steamed up as her crew were waiting for their lunch break.

'Hugo, at last! We are ready no? Jo do you have the new tapes? There's a good girl run up and give them to Steven in the box so we can get on with this. Stand by ladies and gents.'

The piano diagonally faced the audience at the front of the stage, with its keys pointing upstage to hide the mechanics from the audience. Although a fake piano, from the audience it looked surprisingly realistic. The tapes were delivered the lighting dimmed and Hugo took his place at the piano. The sound engineer inserted the cassette and pressed the button to release the voice of Jerry Lee Lewis.

'You shake my nerves and you rattle my brain.'

Across the speakers and Hugo assumed his position of surprise and tried his best to mime to the gritty lyrics. He panicked, as he had not heard the version on the new tape and he hit the first valve that he could, which sent his seat shooting up into the air five foot above the keys. It was a spectacular start.

'I try to call but you're so on fire'.

With his foot Hugo touched what he thought was the valve to return him to the stage level and the lid of the piano shot up, catching him squarely under the chin, knocking him off the stool and releasing a plume of blood from his jaw that cascaded down his white suit jacket. He plummeted downwards to the keyboard, where his face touched the first valve. The piano launched itself, a screaming heap of tubes and woodwork, hissing air and throwing his body across the stage, throwing Hugo to the floor.

'I'm in a spin well it's a sin, Goodness Gracious Great Balls of Fire.'

Throughout this debacle Hugo carried on mouthing the words and looking wide eyed at the audience of technicians and producers. He knew that his job was on the line, yet continued to pull faces while the wound dripped blood on to his costume and seeped its crimson into the weave of his jacket. Climbing back onto the piano, he hit the end keys allowing some control as one leg lifted the piano to a 33-degree angle. He maintained his performance through to the next verse when the stage manager cut the stage lights, put up the working light and called, 'lunch.'

'Bravo, Bravo' called Jean Paul Reme from the auditorium, certain that his protégé had impressed the producers by his antics.

Hugo sat on the piano stool and dared not touch the keys. He had won his place in the production, but knew that he would have to repeat this mayhem each night. Jo walked up behind him and touched his arm, knowing that he had made a successful fool of himself and knowing that she wanted to be with this fool. Alessandro joined them. 'Good Monsieur Hugo, you will be able to do the same each night perhaps?'

Hugo nodded and grinned painfully. 'Zat's showbiz!'

Tambourine dancer

JOEL'S JOURNEY

1983

Joel should wake with the alarm, but he does not this Thursday. He went to bed early and so there's no reason why he would sleep in late. He is still excited about the show and dances the routines, even in sleep.

To the rest of us, this could be any Thursday. We sleep well because there is nothing really for us to get excited about in our tomorrow. We wake up refreshed and then are blighted by the reality of the day ahead. For a lucky few, each day is the opportunity to do what they want. Joel is one of these lucky few. He has been trained to dance and now enjoys the prospect of earning a living from that training. Only today Joel wakes and he is late. He needs to make up time. A creature of habit, he has had this routine set inside him since a child. It is one of the drawbacks for children from the care system. In time Joel will learn to enjoy the chaos that is his freedom.

The clock stopped at 1:46 am and it still says this time, when in reality it is 9:15am. Joel knows that it is late, for when he wakes the sun is too high and too strong. He taps the radio and the true time is announced from the local commercial station. It is O9:16 am.

'Shit!'

He gets out of his bed, washes and dresses not stopping to eat, for there is no time to get any food. The room he sleeps in is also the kitchen. He shares a bathroom with the other members of the house and each occupies a section of the floor space. Every morning each tenant makes a break for the bathroom at the start of the working day and every morning three of them are disappointed and have to wait their turn or start their day unwashed. Joel washes his face in the sink knowing that he will use the shower at work, after the rehearsal. He has been living at this house for the past four months and moved here when the term finished, as it was near to London and near auditions at the end of a short tube ride.

He left Cardiff two years previously to enrol at the Ballet Rambert School, receiving a small grant that had been gifted by the social services. Joel had a talent. He could put his body through angles that were unusual and gymnastically enterprising. A scout from the County Athletics and Sports Council had seen this talent. They took him from the obscurity that is the school gymnasium and he began training and competing for his district of Wales. If you ask him about his start in life, or read his file, he will tell you what he has been told by his social workers. Joel will tell you that he was born in Cardiff, that his mother was a drug user and his father was absent since his conception. There were a few years when he spent time with his mother and he remembers her and someone who he called 'Dad' before an Emergency Protection order took Joel into the care of the local authority. In care, he still had weekly contact with his mother and this continued until he was ten years old, when he was informed of her death. Joel will not talk about this time and he has become accustomed to professionals and charitable persons alike discussing his past as they would a piece of fiction. Joel's past has been shelved since he joined the adult world and he intends never to take a look backwards, lest he repeats one of the chapters. In those years, he began placements with various foster carers who took the young half-caste boy into their homes and, as if his behaviour was on trial, rejected him at the first sign of trouble. He did not show any emotions at these rejections and made 'normalised relationships at school despite the unsettled background', or so his file says.

It is 9:23 am. Joel grabs at an apple from the plywood dresser and jumps into a tracksuit that he keeps for best. His hair is a mess but he prefers it that way. Within ten minutes he will be out of the front door in Tuffnel Park and walking towards the tube station.

Joel was found a placement when he reached 11 years old. It was outside Cardiff in a coastal village called Lavernock Point. The family were commissioned by the social services as foster carers and also ran a caravan site over-looking the bay. They appeared to the young Joel, to have the perfect family with two grown up children and time to lavish on the young boy. Joel lived with May and Charlie for three years and for those years, had joined that family.

Joel leaves the flat. He carries his dance shoes and a roll of papers that have the production schedule written upon them. In his pocket are his wallet, cigarettes and Walkman. He walks southwards to the tube station. Beyond Camden Town there are many sections of terraced houses that make up the old suburbs. This area of North London has become converted to cheap private rental properties. Tuffnel Park is one of these suburbs and offers cheap housing with access to transport links.

When Joel's foster parents handed him back, they did not do so with the complaints that he was unruly or disturbed. They found in him a gentle spirit who quickly assimilated into the family until he was 14 years old. They handed him back only because his foster mother, May, became ill and when they knew there was little hope of her recovery, the department thought that it would be better to remove him to another placement rather than impose a foster child on the family during their time of impending grief. There was no other placement, so Joel returned to Cardiff and he was taken into a care home where he remained until his sixteenth year. Joel can read this in his file, or he can look in the memory book, which his social worker prepared for him. The book includes pictures and letters from those he loved as well as those he never knew. He has pictures of his holidays and Christmas, with May and Charlie and a few mementos of their family. There is even a photograph of his mother looking well and this is the picture he keeps in his wallet. It was while he was at the children's home that he started showing the abilities in sport, especially the indoor gymnasium. May had seen his potential as an athlete and encouraged him to join a youth group in the local leisure centre. In He had a natural sense of poise and, despite the dangers would walk along bars and walls regardless of his safety, confident that he would not fall.

Joel turns out of his street and down to the station. It is a quick walk; his pace is brisk, as he is late. The morning is crisp, but promises as it does in June, to warm uncomfortably. He stops at a local newsagent and buys a bottle of milk, which he finishes before he reaches the station and leaves on a wall outside the tube station for someone to break later. He has a travel pass and walks through the ticket barrier waving his authority with the pride that he can afford to pay his way.

He moved back into the care of the rowdy children's home and was placed on an Interim Care Order that became permanent. Joel accepted the change to his life and spent as much time controlling the one element he could, his body. The school gave him access to sports materials and gym equipment and he spent each evening in activities. He could make his body move and shape exactly as he wished. It did not argue back, except for the burning muscular flesh that could be eased in a later shower.

Joel travels down the escalator to the platform and reads the pictures on the tiled walls depicting sanitary products and new chocolate bars. There is a theatrical poster of Alessandro advertising the show in which Joel is appearing. The picture shows Alessandro in free flight over an astonished audience. Joel has a small part in this show and dances each night for the minimum Equity wage.

Joel was never destined for the Olympic stadiums. Although his skills were county and even national standard they were lacking one element which held him back. The county coach had suggested that he work in the indoor floor teams, and he mastered the agility tests but was lacking any flair. While the girls would dance their routines to a musical score, the boys had to swing and rotate to the gritty silence that is considered masculine. When Joel saw and heard the girls dancing to music, he recognised what was missing for him. His moves only felt complete when there was sound to lift them. Then he would jump higher and push further with the music supporting him. Male dancers are a rare find and Joel's sports teachers wisely channelled this young boy away from the discipline of gymnastics into the study of dance. When he reached 16 years old, he knows not how, or who made the call, but he was offered an audition with the Ballet Rambert School. He did not know of this institution or what the audition entailed, but he went all the same. After a gruelling day in a studio in Southwest London accompanied by his social worker, he was offered a place and accepted it without question. The Cardiff County provided him with a full scholarship and arranged all his practical needs. For two years Joel enjoyed the study and his identity as an adult formed. In those years he found a family in dance and is now a member of that professional body that has welcomed his talents.

Joel mentally calculates the train is due in three minutes. For those three minutes he puts the headphones to his ears and plays a tape, tapping his feet in response to the synthesized rhythms playing. He looks at his watch and begins counting back the minutes he will need to get to the rehearsals on time. The train will be in the station in three minutes. It is a five-minute journey and then a five-minute jog trot to the theatre. Joel will make it by ten. Inside the theatre it is now 9:30 am and the company have already assembled for the emergency rehearsal that all, except Joel, have remembered. Pedro is a stickler for time keeping. Pedro is the Spanish choreographer for the 'Tambourine number', which is on today's schedule. He says, through his translator that 'time keeping is the essence of dance and should be the first rule of the professional'. The missing dancer holds up the rehearsals and when a role call is taken, it is Joel who has not shown up for work. On the train Joel is listening to his music, lost in the pulsating metronome that is the core of contemporary 80's pop. He has bought the Walkman with his wages that is a new device on at the cutting edge of personal entertainment. When he left the Rambert School there was no guarantee of work and he has been luckier than some on his course, for he has found a dance job and can fulfil his training. The rehearsal today is a recap. The show opened two weeks ago, but the Tambourine number has not been going well in the estimation of the producers. On Wednesday night the scene fell apart. The audience chuckled when they should have wowed and the final set piece did not work. Pedro was incensed that his contribution to the show was a fiasco, and called everyone to extra rehearsal, in an attempt drill competence in to his creation. Some of the show works and other sections are clumsily executed. What works for a French audience might not be appropriate for the London crowds and Pedro's reputation and meal ticket are resting on this rehearsal. If the Tambourine scene does not impress the producers it will be replaced by another 'girl on girl' floorshow and Pedro will be sent back to Paris a failure. Joel is missing and now has been identified.

Joel's speciality is as an acrobat who dances. He excels when he flies through the air and his own muscle control defies gravity for several stunning seconds. He however finds the banging of a tambourine to a second rate Spanish pop tune, not an easy task. Where the Rambert School taught free expression through the movement of the body, Pedro demands that the dancers hit the tambourine at the same time without any expression other than a fixed grimace. The dance has been in Pedro's family for centuries and most of the cast wished he had kept it with them rather than sharing it with London. Pedro blames the slack English dancers, who he says are 'patting his noble instrument when it should be banged like two bodies in passion.' There are a number of the dancers who think that this section of the show is amateurish this has led to a suicidal performance, best described as 'Twenty-five lemmings breaking into the school percussion cupboard'. At the end of the routine Joel performs a back flip, kicking one of the tambourines into the air, it is the only part he likes and he is the only one in the company to successfully perform the stunt. Because he is the only dancer who can perform this part of the act, he is a necessary element to this rehearsal and noticeably missing.

At Leicester Square tube, Joel races up the escalator and darts between the tiled corridors until he reaches the central hub of the station. Leicester Square North side is the exit and he is familiar with the quickest route to the theatre. He will cut through Leicester Square then up past the Swiss Centre through China Town into Denman Street and the Regent Theatre.

At the foot of Denman Street is a café that makes snacks with Joel's favourite bread, a bacon sandwich that will sustain him through the long rehearsal. He stops most mornings at this cafe and has been eating well to keep up his energy. Mirrored in the shop window he sees his body looking strong and muscular, his shoulders are shaped and he has a stomach, on which he can bounce pennies. He likes his mixed race status, and being black in London feels easy compared to his childhood in Wales.

In May's family he felt he was always the only black face in his community and a mixture of two cultures. His mother was white and he can sometimes remember her face. His memory is a picture, like the photograph given to him with her effects, but she was more beautiful than he could ever be. His face does not fit his body. He has lived with his changing features all his life and like most children did not ever consider himself to be pleasing to the eye and does not remember anyone saying so to him. As he matured, his face grew disproportionate to his Grecian physique, giving him the look of a deformed Bull over a man's body. His self-image makes him painfully shy around sexual partners and he still has not ventured into a relationship in case he is truly discovered for the monster he believes he sees before him.

Paying for the food, Joel walks up the concreted pathway to the small entrance at the side of the Regent Theatre, eating his breakfast. Prudie is inside reading a magazine and is surprised to see a straggler passing her door. Joel is now half an hour late for Pedro's rehearsal. She shows him the call sheet and his memory is jolted. There is no excuse; Joel has simply forgotten that he was meant to be there for 9:30am. He drops his sandwich on the ledge of the stage door window and hurtles down to the stage level. As he opens the thick oak doors to the gloom, he hears 24 tambourines all breaking the silence in a disarray of incompetence. This is followed by the screams in Spanish and simultaneous translation into English and French by the army of linguists employed to share expletives with this mixture of performers. In the auditorium the producers sit in the darkness smoking and discussing the merits of cutting this item from their show. Their occasional comments enrage Pedro, who re-directs his anger at his dancers, who in turn fall at the first musical fence. Joel hovers at the side of the stage. He wants to take his place, he wants the scene to be cut, but he knows that by walking on to the stage he will be shamed and risk losing his reputation in front of, not just his colleagues, but also the management who pay his wages.

His fear of Pedro and the Producers' loosens his stomach in a physical sense of despair. The languages twist him and confuse his hungry, sleep-deprived mind. Joel begins to fall and before his legs go and he collapses in the blackness of the wings, he feels a hand touch his shoulder. A white painted face catches the light from the prompt desk. It is Alessandro, the star of the show who has never spoken to him other than as a member of the chorus. Alessandro had noticed him in the chorus line and was attracted to this boy's beautiful, grotesque look. Alessandro calls Joel the 'Minotaur' when describing him to others. It is a cruel name that he would never say to his face. Alessandro dislikes the scene as much as he loathes Pedro and takes every opportunity to undermine Pedro and his choreography. Taking his little 'Greek Monster' on to the stage with him Alessandro starts up an imaginary conversation in mid-flow.

'. . . It was as I was saying last night . . . the scene is better viewed from the Circle. Ah Pedro, gentlemen, fellow performers, we, I mean I, for I have requisitioned this young person from your midst, I apologise for the delay in our attendance. My friend and I were upstairs where Joel was showing me the technicalities of the steps and we just forgot time. My dear friend Pedro, I wished to play a part in this traditional dance in our production, but could not bear to embarrass myself without first mastering your steps.' Alessandro launched into a rendition of the dance perfectly positioned and stable . . . you see my young friend has taught me well, thank you Joel, thank you'.

At this he gives the dancer a knowing wink and steps aside as Pedro reconvened the routine with the full 25 dancers in position. Nothing more was said and both Pedro's ego and Joel's reputation were saved for another day.

Joel danced as if his feet contained helium and the scene started to shape into a performance. After an hour Pedro turned to his producers satisfied that he had turned these dancers to a near perfect display. He presented Joel to the directors' as his 'special ingredient,' proclaiming in Spanish that the scene was now a triumph and that it needed the boy with a 'face like a bull,' to make it work. To this day Joel is affectionately known as the 'The Minotaur' and accepts that name, as it is a small price to pay for his gift.

FOR A CHILD NEVER KNOWN

2006

'I have no photograph of my mother or father. I just have a picture in my mind so they are not gone from my memory. You also have nothing of your father, so I shall give you that memory' . . .

1983

They rolled over, one black, one white and after they had finished making love, and in their individual stilted broken languages, started asking the personal questions that lovers usually do when they have missed out a long courtship. She had never been outside the central London area, which she had made her home during the run of the musical. In Paris, she would travel anywhere without care, knowing every corner of her capital. When she lived in Angola, she knew the bush and the surrounding village, for the walk to fetch water required that she travel the two miles to the well twice a day to carry for her own and her family's survival. She now indulges herself with water and bathing is her greatest luxury. She feels the corner of the bed and touches his skin, his white flesh undulating over a thin frame, twitches as he sleeps and she settles herself. She has no knowledge of where in London they are. The minicab that took them home drove for a full half hour through dark streets and linked one late night fast food outlet to another until they stopped outside his house. That was the night. That was their only night. They had kissed in the theatre, his mouth pressing urgently to hers before he asked her to come home with him. They kissed in the taxi, when she touched his face. She was happy to have him for the night, this night.

When she arrived in London with the other model the choreographer asked her what she could do.

'Do?' she had exclaimed in French, for she spoke no English, 'I stand and am beautiful.'

In the show she does just this. She stands in a costume that has feathers and silks that twinkle with a thousand diamond stones. She is beautiful. She is beautiful dressed, and she was more beautiful naked! When the choreographer asked, 'What do you expect to get from London?' She replied in a matter of fact way, pointing across the stage towards the Props boy, 'I want to do him!'

The prop boy was called over by the choreographer during notes and in front of the chorus told that he was on a promise, just in case he might be interested in expanding his experience. The dancer's found the comment hysterical and treated him as piece of young meat he was, yet he did not forget and after one show when he rejected his lover, the props boy surprised the dark beautiful girl in the auditorium and kissed her. His lips found hers, not as a greeting but with intent for a more developed exploration and she went with him. She took the boy's hand and they left the theatre together, and in the darkness of the minicab they sat awkwardly awaiting their first sex. She had been planning to go to her own home and had not thought that she would be travelling across London with a potential new lover. There is an excitement to making love for the first time, for there is never a guarantee but the boy was on a promise. The taxi stopped outside a ramshackle residential block. The boy and the model went up the stairs to the front door. From the dingy hallway, he ushered her into his bedroom, where they shed their clothes. He was still sweating from the show and said he wanted a shower. She joined him and they ran hand in hand, naked mono-chromed together across the landing, to the bathroom. They made love with the water covering their bodies in a film of heat and soap.

There were of different textures and hairlines, the mixed colours of their skins adding into one harmonious mix of release. After they dried and fell into his bed, they entered each other again, lovemaking until he fell asleep. She watched him dreaming and saw the image that she found beautiful. She, who each night had projected her beauty on the stage, knew that looks pass, and must be appreciated while they last. In the morning they woke, separately wondering where they had left their clothes and a little ashamed of the limp smelling bodies and sleepy breath. They tried to speak to each other, she in her broken English, and he with what he could remember from his school French. She got up naked in front of him and from her handbag took a tub of butter oil, which she rubbed into her legs and buttocks. He watched as she explained to him in fluent French that she was trying to slow down the ageing process and needed to preserve her skin's softness by replenishing the essential oils in her tanned body. He did not understand the words she spoke, but lay in the bed absorbed in the spectacle as she touched herself. She liked being the centre of his attention, as if he knew what she was saying.

They ate a little breakfast in a kitchen with the housemates, all sitting at the table nudging and wide-eyed at the boy's newest conquest and he introduced them to Claire. She felt exotic and out of place and wondered what they were going to say when she left. He took her back on the underground train to her home in Central London, where he kissed her. He said that she was beautiful and it had been a beautiful night and that he was still in love with someone else. So they never spent another night like that one. They worked together for a few more weeks and then she returned to Paris, where the child was born.

'That was the night and you are the beautiful daughter that came from that night.

DOMINIC'S HORIZONS

1983

Dominic is now a waiter, even though he spent three years at a London drama academy and has achieved the award for 'Most Promising Radio Voice 1981', he is a waiter. When he graduated, he was awarded rave reviews and was considered the student with the 'most promising future' for his year class. Two agents actually bid to represent him at his graduation performance, based upon his portrayal of Sir Toby Belch, a part that he took over at a week's notice from a student with laryngitis. He was envied by his peers but also respected for his engaging manner offstage. The promising career of any young actor is never guaranteed. After all the hype awarded to him, Dominic had still not worked since he graduated after eight months. He took catering jobs because he had to support his bed-sit home and his grant only lasted until his graduation. His prospects had not lived up to the expectation of his academy and the pearl that was his promised future, was still in its shell and clinging doggedly to the seabed. He believed, as do most outside the industry that once a performer has been discovered and issued with a first Equity contract, the career path is laid.

The actor and dancer are not as secure as one might believe, for each contract they earn, though the audition process has a short life and becomes their last piece of work. If they expect further employment they have to restart the process of application, impression and confidence that rewarded them previously. Most of the time they are employed they are worrying about the impending unemployment ahead and they are forever searching for the next job. What are these rewards that make a person want to give up the security of a normal working life? Is it the moments of audience adulation, the chance of celebrity, or an opportunity to work alongside the greats performers of the theatre? Is to be a part of the old masters of literature and the new voices of tomorrow that are enough for the young theatrical applicant to be so regularly hungry and disappointed? There must be some reason for this calling, as thousands of hopefuls pitch themselves into this dream with only a few of the lucky and dedicated, who see though to a training and career. Even when they are ready to join the audition line, only through constant determined pursuit of their career, can a performer expect to make a moderate living. Noel Coward was right to warn mothers for putting a daughter on the stage, for very few of those sons and daughters will find that platform, and those who do get there will be constantly fear falling from it.

    Being a waiter was Dominic's only career option, as it allowed him time to attend auditions and provided him with an income, but he never gave up hope. Dominic still had his dreams and would spend every Thursday close reading the advertisements in 'The Stage', in the hope that there might be an audition that does not stipulate union membership. After reading one advert, he applied for an audition. The advertisement called for, 'Actors/Actresses and Dancers for New French Spectacular, to perform waiting duties and appear in a musical number in the performance.' This waiting job was the nearest he had ever been to a working theatre and after eight months on the scrapheap, he was successfully auditioned and accepted the position. The French directors believed that by mixing the waiters with the show they were breaking down the third wall that divides the stage from the auditorium. When your table waiter breaks into song, the audience is connected to the performers, the waiter becoming a conduit to the magical world on the stage. It was a novel idea to integrate stage and auditorium and worked well in Paris, but the French did not consider the reserve of the London Theatre-goer. Despite warnings from the English Producer, Michael Leighton, staff contracts were issued and auditions held before an application was made to the professional actors union. A special dispensation was eventually granted from Equity, who allowed the waiting staff to join the cast but they insisted on certain conditions. Equity, the actors' union operated a closed shop, so anyone who performed in the West End had to be a full Equity member. To appear on a West End stage, Equity insisted that although the singing waiters could join in with the artistes', they were not to interact physically with the stage, or the company. To prevent any integration, an imagined barrier operated across the front of the curtain line. The waiters were not to pass this point during the show and the cast were to report any infringement of this ruling to their union representative. Dominic was caught in this catch 22 situation of unionisation. Even with his training, he was unable to get a union card as he needed to be working to receive a nomination, and he could only get a nomination if he was working. Since each production company only had one card placement to offer a year, there was immense competition for these places and made it near impossible, for a young talent to be launched. The French directors did not believe in union's authority, or understand the point of a closed shop membership; they just wanted to mix the two groups. So to please the union, they installed a lift that elevated the waiters to just below the stage level, keeping them separated by inches from the legitimate artistes above.

Dominic became one of thirty waiters and he was at the bottom of that group. There was a headwaiter, Charles, and it is he who has been given the position above the waiting staff and had appointed lieutenants to keep an eye on them. The headwaiter was like the chorus master across the line; he dressed with a little extra style, had a better wage, did not have to wait tables and had the ear of his masters. He had confidence and belief in himself, considering that he had more talent, which he thought would project him one day across the line to become a cast member. Part of this belief and confidence stemmed from his being stupid and vain, and the other reason was that he has slept with the show's star and considered this to be his dream ticket. In the work environment, Dominic's indifference to Charles and his subordinates angered this queen bee and consequently Dominic was constantly singled out for menial tasks in an attempt to break his spirit. Dominic's entry into the profession meant him starting at the bottom of a very long chain. A chain, to which Dominic was unwittingly linked, choking his future. The theatre industry is hierarchical. The waiters are the lowest ends of the catering team they are not skilled like the chefs and are despised by those they serve. As the theatre has developed into a restaurant, the company employed this army of waiting staff, many of whom had aspirations to tread the boards rather than serve the tables. During the rehearsals, the catering and waiting staffs were drilled by the headwaiter who, insisted on a similar regime of discipline he saw in the Chorus line. They learned to carry the plates, 'just so' and serve in a flamboyant, camp way that he believed was much more entertaining than the traditional 'silver service'. The cast rehearsed the final routines and so did the waiters, yet neither of the two groups were allowed to meet during the rehearsals. The cast had allocated dressing rooms and began to plaster them with temporary adornments to make their work place seem more like their theatrical home. The waiters got a locker in a corridor and had to pay a deposit on the key.

The evening show provided a full three-course meal with plenty of expensive alcoholic drinks served at inflated prices. This was followed by a cabaret with disco that did not finish until the early hours, which made their hours long. The scene in which the 'waiting staff' joined the stage performers, took place through the main food course. The waiters had to learn a song, yet were only expected to mime perfectly to the music. It was a turgid ditty written especially for the occasion but, like a 'music worm' etched its way into the brain and regularly regurgitated its tune. Day by day, Dominic resented the song, the people, his need to work, and his true career which, he realised was slipping further from his grasp. As the song was sung, the waiters were supposed to leave their post and line up on the forestage. In the second verse Alessandro, the show's star, sprinkled magic dust over them, as the mechanical stage lift rose. The stage gently projected the waiters to just below the stage level and the cast, the collective mass of 'black tied robots' swaying in time to the music, singing of a wish to take flight like the master before them. Dominic lived this humiliation each performance, after three years at a premier drama school he had aspirations to being more than a singing waiter.

To keep sanity, he began to write little, observations at first and then monologues that were fine parodies of the world around him. On Sundays, when the theatre had its one night of sleep, Dominic attended a pub comedy night and tried out this material on the late-night drinking fraternity. In his comic monologue, Dominic described the effeminacy he saw as becoming the popular culture. He showed how, in reality, 'Camp-ness' can be misogynistic, puerile and bigoted. He used all his observations to channel his audience's opinions and then draw humour from his conclusions. His words were thought provoking, but also very sharp and funny. He used all his skills and drama training to present these thoughts lucidly and he found a voice to play to the audiences. Each week Dominic wrote more material and each week he began to find his feet as a performer on another stage.

The French show opened and the waiting work was full on for Dominic and the other robots. They did not have time to think, as working six days out of the seven made little time for much else. Charles called rehearsals in the upstairs bar and his feathers became more puffed up each day, as he believed that he was elevated to a position of their director. It was now common knowledge that he was sleeping with Alessandro and this had inflated Charles's ego to the annoyance of his underlings. The Headwaiter copied his lover by plastering his face with theatrical make up, as a mask to his evil. He spread his venom across those he had beneath him and insisted that all the waiter's use cosmetic enhancements as part of their costume. The regime was hard for some and waiters left in tears never to return, replaced by other waiters, whom Charles had personally chosen for his entourage. Dominic still kept his outside performances hidden from his employer and continued his solo act every Sunday night, taking his ideas to other venues on the comedy circuit and building his reputation. Then a letter arrived from one of these clubs telling Dominic he had been selected as a best comedy newcomer. The prize was a gig at one of London's most prestigious comedy venues that had a reputation to be the preferred place of the television scouts. He could not tell any of his colleagues about this opportunity and quietly put his clothing away on the night of the gig, in his hurry to escape. After the Saturday night show, he ran from the theatre through Leicester Square towards the river. It took him five minutes passing down the side of Charing Cross Station the clock at the station showing it was 1am. The gig had already started, but he was not on until last. As Dominic stepped into the club, he met the compére.

'You're late and you're on.'

His introduction warmed the crowd before he got into the main thrust of his patter. The audience were with him through the whole act and laughed exactly as Dominic had directed them to laugh. Some wondered about his strange make up, but assumed it to be an ironic statement. He finished his set and the club went wild. Ushered off to great applause he was taken to an antichamber, where he was given a drink and congratulated. In the mass of acolytes there were two faces he recognised. Alessandro and Charles stood in front of him. Alessandro was gracious while Charles had the face of a sucked lemon. Dominic nodded as Alessandro spoke to him for the first time.

'So it was you, my little friend. I wondered if you might have seen us in the balcony. You are how is it you say, Charles, 'sublime,' yes; you amused me a great deal. You must come to a little gathering next Sunday at Julian and Francine's and you can entertain us there.'

Dominic was deflated that Alessandro and the headwaiter had found out his secret and he expected to be humiliated further. Charles flicked a card in Dominic's direction with the address of the producer's home and a time to arrive where he knew he would be expected to sing for his supper.

That Sunday, Dominic did attend the party as directed on the card and was surprised to be greeted at the Chelsea home by Charles, who even on a weekend sported his uniform. Charles appeared to be acting, as the producer's butler and inching his way into the crack that he hoped would be his step up the performance ladder.

'Well, well, Dominic isn't it? Welcome to one of our events. You were quite a hit with Alessandro at the club the other night. He wanted to invite you to this gathering and I thought that it would be a good idea for you to see how you could progress. I have told Alessandro how I have been grooming you and he thinks that he can possibly make something of out your little performance. We shall see.'

Charles did not wait for a reply and strolled off towards a group at the other end of the reception room. Dominic looked about him. There were cast members and a few minor celebrities standing with glasses of champagne and talking in various European languages he couldn't decipher. Outside in the garden, he could see the tanned bodies of the prettiest dancers from the chorus, diving into the cool personalised waters of the swimming pool. The house was filled with glamorous men and women, none over thirty and all in their best outfits. Alessandro was talking to a short, dark, hairy woman and a man in a blue sports jacket and matching glasses. Seeing Dominic in the distance, he made his excuses and walked towards Charles and the young comic, ready to welcome the waiter into this new world. Before he greeted the newcomer, Charles turned and whispered in Dominic's ear, 'Tell me waiter, what is it like to be an after thought?'

OLD ROCKERS NEVER DIE

1983

A power chord cuts through the auditorium. On stage, clouds, generated by the smoke machines swirl around the band as the bass drum starts a backbeat. Zute Graff stands tall as the curtain rises. Tracie stands at his side, arms stretched out screeching the opening refrain. The other musicians take position, their instruments at a volume that will pound their audience. If I were to paint a portrait of a Rock Legend, it would be Zute, tall and wiry, smoke folding around his legs, his body shaping the mist with the guitar, calling out to his fans that he is their leader.

He is hungry for the attention and desperate to succeed, for it is the break the band deserve and find so hard to achieve. Zute, and the band, have been working the clubs since the late seventies and have always had near misses. He will tell you that he has met and sung alongside the famous. He has missed out on recording contracts, deals and promotional opportunities, for no other reason than fate's cruel hand. He never made it to stadiums, yet he has supported top bands as they rose to break the stratosphere. Zute has remained on ground level and turned his failure into anger. He still has the self-belief that he will join the successful. He will not entertain being told he has missed the boat or is washed up, and believes he sings as well as he did when he was eighteen, and was first heard by Hendrix. He will tell anyone who listens he could have joined the band 'The Sweet', but did not like their outfits and later he turned down an offer from Spandau Ballet because he never understood the band's name.

The Producers have agreed to listen to the Zute Graf band and may consider them for a regular late night slot in this West End venue. It would be a great showcase for Zute.

So Zute stands on the stage. He feels at home here surrounded by lights and intense sound. He has given Tracie one number to sing that leaves him free to play the lead guitar solo on his Gibson Les Paul original, an instrument that he is paying off by working weekends for a bookie in Camden. For years they have played the clubs around the UK, travelling in their black rusted transit van, totalling thousands of miles in the search of a few fans. They have always believed in a brighter future and when they stop believing then they will stop playing.

Zute finishes his first verse and Tracie gives the answer call and chorus riff to his melodic guitar lead. She is over twenty years his junior and looks at him as she sings, her eyes melting with dirty passion. Hers is a truly special voice. Zute's voice is toned through his years of abuse and at thirty-eight he has started the decline for a rock musician, time gently nudging him into the place where all old rockers end. He lives in Camden Lock, in a small flat after he came down from Peterborough in the late sixties and has lived in the same small space because he hates the planning needed to move. Tracie has been with Zute for a couple of years since she herself came to London. She has lost most of her Ipswich accent and tries to model herself on Debbie Harry. She waits tables during the day at the swanky Criterion café bar in Piccadilly. At seventeen years old she cannot work at the bar or serve drinks, but she has a false I.D. Tracie dreams of a recording career and unlike her lover she has her youth and a voice that could unlock the pop market she craves. Zute knows her voice has potential, yet he cannot admit she could eclipse him one day.

Julian has suggested that to raise the profile of the Regent Cabaret show, they should change the type of clientele that visit the theatre. Gone are the sweet singing cabaret voices that chirp innocently the old, standard hits, these are supplanted by the new wave of young performers who will fill the theatre after the pubs close. He sees Tracie as a Siren, and is willing to back the songbird. Julian and Francine discovered Tracie in a restaurant. They asked her what the young people like to see late at night and she said that she and her boyfriend go to watch new bands. Tracie said that she knew of a great band, as she was really a singer and not a waitress. Julian asked for her number and then called her to arrange an audition, as he was intrigued by the girl's forthright nature. It gave Julian a thrill that he could hold a young person's attention by his ability to make their futures. He never tires of this power and since becoming a producer, he never uses that power well.

The second song begins slowly. Tracie's voice is a power machine that can project sound to the back of a person's mind. Its sensitivity raises the hair on the backs of a listener's neck, a physical act, which is an emotional response to her talent. The song has a tenderness that is beyond the vocalist's young age but she carries the emotional text with maturity. Zute wrote the song for her and he watches Tracie's as she sings out the lyrics with precise intonation to the few audience members judging them. He takes the reins of leadership for the final three songs, Tracie now only making a contribution to the harmonies, yet she alone is holding Julian's attention. After they have played five numbers Julian comes to the front of stage and asks to speak to Zute and Tracie. The band, pack up their equipment and are shown to the stage door by Jo, the deputy stage manager who has elected to work the afternoon audition.

'I will give you a week,' said Julian appeasing the rock musician, 'and I want the girl to sing in the show.'

Zute is happy to accept any conditions and the money is agreed at three times the usual gigging rate, together with an assurance that Zute can invite any professional promoters he wishes to his performances.

They leave the theatre high on their success. The rest of the band, climb into their battered Transit van to take the equipment back to their flats, while Zute and Tracie walk back towards Camden, preferring the London air to the crews banter. Zute has not registered Julian's request for Tracie to appear in his show and believes himself, to have secured the booking. Tracy wonders how she will tell him that she is now going to have to quit her job in the restaurant, for she does not want to appear to be stealing his thunder.

'They want the band!' says the musician. Zute is on his cloud and is not coming down for anyone. He took a 'tab' from his own stock before they left the theatre and he is already 'high'. Zute has a life living with drugs.

He deals in the nightclubs. He and Tracie have a network that covers North London from Islington to Euston, limiting his stock to amphetamine and the cannabis resins. He has become acquainted with many in the music world, yet none have ever taken him seriously as a musician since he is their dealer. He is not a regular user himself, claiming that he is not the type of person who has an addictive personality, yet he has never had a really clean week since arriving in London. There is always a market for the drugs that he can supply, and he does have his rent to pay. They walk the three miles back to Camden, through the West End. Neon's blaze opportunity, advertising the world of the night and things the couple would soon aspire to purchase. Zute has always loved the night; his day often begins after the setting sun and closes when the milkman chinks his morning welcome. Tracie's dreams are for the same recognition, and she is closer to realizing her hopes than her lover is to his. Zute steps haphazardly, avoiding the gaps in the paving cracks, a habit he still keeps from his childhood. They traverse the Euston Road, a bleak wasteland that cuts the chic West End from the north of the city. Neither feels they are Londoners and yet they will probably never leave. They cross the fast road, cheating death between the fast moving boxes of steel that cut east to west. At the tube station they walk to the edge of the canal and amble amongst the closed market stalls. In the daytime, Tracie often walks through the stalls fingering the cheap trinkets stealing when she can. She only buys what Zute lets her, as he needs her wages. They reach the alley that separates two warehouses from the lock Zute leads his mistress forcibly up an iron stairway to a battered door and he turns the lock with a single click. Zute can only think of his own future. 'They want the band!'

He walks into the flat, ignoring Tracie, who keeps a pace or two behind him. He goes to the fridge and, dropping the keys on the table, opens the white door to let the spotlight flush his face. 'Getting used to the light already!'

He pulls out a beer and in one hand, opens the can and puts it to his opening mouth. Tracie removes her shoes, takes the band from her hair and lets the peroxide blonde fall across her shoulders. Zute sits at the table littered with washing up and chip papers. He puts the beer down on the table and beckons her over to him. She says nothing but like an automaton walks over and stands in front of him. He grabs her hands and in one swing pulls her round so she falls into his lap. His breath, cool from the beer, touches her face as their lips meet. When they separate, the thin line of wet holds them together for a second, before breaking as she smiles. His face is cold and he knows that her light is brighter than his.

'Say it,' he says, "say it.'

'I love . . . ' she says automatically. 'I love you Daddy!'

THE DANCER

2006

Ellen takes a pill; she is not sure what this one does. They are new.

She has written to James in France, explaining some of her thoughts and the prognosis. James and Eloise intend to set up a therapy centre, for the local spa waters offer a relief for many ailments. She knows she is not be welcome there but could certainly benefit from the treatments.

Jack walks in and, ignoring his mother, opens the fridge and drinks from a juice bottle. His head nods in time with the 'tishing' sounds coming from his headphones. Ellen tries to talk to Jack and he walks off without saying anything. She hears him clump upstairs, the door slams and then from the powerful stereo in Jack's bedroom, 'Green Day' starts removing the plaster from the walls.

The phone rings and it is her mother's weekly call. She wants to tell her. She wants to let her mother know that disabled people get cancer too.

'You'll visit soon?' she hears herself say.

These past weeks Ellen has been planning. The problem that she finds with her mobility, compared to walkers, is that everything needs to be second-guessed and arranged. She has thought about the future. Jack will get over her. They have a practical relationship.

He shows his love for her is shown in many ways, just as his father did, and she knows that he will be strong when her death comes. James is close to his son; they share the mobility that Ellen has lacked all Jack's life. Since there are no videos of Ellen dancing, or even walking, the only image Jack has of his mother is with wheels at her side. There might be an old show tape; she could ask Denny at the reunion. Ellen hopes that Jack will go to France with his father, or they could all move back to this house. Ellen has views about how funerals will work. The Catholic tradition will do, as it will be for the family and they will need something to blame. It is a good way of filling the church and Ellen always works best to a full house. She wants to have her coffin placed on a trolley made from wheelchair parts and pushed up the aisle to the sound track of 'I could have danced all night'. That is a way off yet.

Ellen is letting go of her life, just as she let go of her dance. She has other things to worry about and the re-union is just one on the list. It would be playing to the cheap seats to break the news to her old colleagues when they are out for a fun afternoon. How should she tell everyone about this latest kick, when she is already pitied?

'Oh and by the way I won't be making it next year, bloody cancer!'

Denny in her saintly mode would be almost unbearable. The old colleagues will all be shocked, yet slightly relieved that the finger has pointed at someone else and they will all make banal statements of support that will equal nothing, for they cannot share her disease.

The plus side to the diagnosis is that she has some time to make plans. She will ask James to live back at the house with Eloise. They could look after Jack in the home he has always known and she could watch over them all. Just like a Mrs De Winter at her Manderlay. Her sense of humour becomes very dark when she thinks too much and there's a dinner to cook for Jack.

Mandy at Lunch

A KISS GOODBYE

1983

Mandy has talent. She is sure on her feet and sings on cue like an angel,

She exercises her voice before every performance, looks after her body, neither smokes nor drinks to excess and will only stay up partying if she has no show the following day. Her strongest selling point is that she is 'punctual, prompt and perky'. 'Mandy', it says in the programme has been 'dancing since the age of five and trained at the Guildhall School of Music'. She is now thirty years old and her future career will be built on a reputation for these qualities, as well as her talent.

Michael Leighton played back the videotape he shot during the previous week's shows, so that Julian and Francine could see Mandy always turning in one of her consistently good performances. As the Francine and Julian watch the same girl repeating the same moves precisely each night, Michael points out how her consistency benefits the show.

'Consecutive nights and she stands,' he freezes the tape, 'exactly on the same spot, see? I marked the stage. This is why we need to keep her! She never lets you down and sets the benchmark to the rest of the chorus.'

There were decisions to be made. Julian and Francine had decided that Mandy, the current female lead vocalist in the show, was to be superseded by a younger model, which they already had hired, without consulting anyone. Michael cannot believe that they are going to sack her.

'Mandy has been with the company for the past four months. Since the show opened, she has not missed a performance. You cannot seriously think about replacing her!' Michael pleaded.

'We are tired of her face and so is the audience,' answered Julian. 'It's an average performance. We need to have the audiences wowed not just entertained by this, a cruise ship singer.'

The English producer tried again, appealing to the French couple financing this production that there was more to casting, than hiring and firing whenever they felt bored with a performer. The French had made an art of cancelling a finished scene, because it felt wrong one night, or discarding a hugely expensive set because they had changed their minds. It was a costly way to run a business.

'Who have you thought would replace her,' asked Michael Leighton sarcastically.

Julian looked over his large blue-rimmed spectacles at Francine, who nodded back at him, her agreement to tell.

'We have engaged a young singer who we think typifies the current musical trends. Mandy has a fine voice and the number she sings is fine also, but it is all too safe. We need a little, unexpected magic!'

'Piaf!' exclaimed Francine,

'We need someone vulnerable, who will win the hearts of the people each night!' continued Julian.

The Englishman bowed to the paymasters. Mandy would be removed and their new 'Piaf' would take her place. It was, after all, their money. Michael himself had lost his heart to Mandy. Her voice had bewitched him. She was his 'Sparrow', vulnerable and cherished. He had become accustomed to seeing her each night and believed she sang to him personally.

Michael left the couple's house in Chelsea and walked up to the Kings Road to hail a cab. He saw a number 14 bus, coming up towards him and since it stopped by his side he got on.

From the top deck he saw a different view to that from a taxicab. Because he does not drive, he has always relied on others to deliver him to his next appointment. He did not like the tube as he found it claustrophobic, so it was either the bus, or a taxi, that transported him around London. Since his recent success, he prefers the extra expense of a cab, against the economy of the omnibus. Michael is the son of a theatrical Lord of the Realm and has a matriarch who has had books and plays written about her and her sisters. He has immaculate tastes in clothing, which he inherited from his father's tailor and can sense a production on the rocks. Michael's father approves of his sons running of the family business, as he was born to handle the family firm. He has proved to be sensible with the business and has held off investing any of his own money in this production. Each week it lingers, the more pleased he is that he has not committed his family to this project.

He has arranged to meet with Mandy at 'The Fountain Room' in Fortnum and Mason on Piccadilly, prior to a rehearsal. When he left the French couple to their lunch, he agreed that he would be the one to dismiss her as the vocalist in the show, just as he has been commissioned to sack other reliable talents. Only this time, he is dreading the effect it will have on himself. While he bumps along on the Kings Road, he thinks about what other opportunities he can make for Mandy, with which to appease her disappointment. Mandy was thrilled when she was offered the part and had, for four months, served the show professionally. Privately, their friendship has grown to a selection of expensive suppers and during these evenings out, Michael had begun to think that he might have found someone with whom he could consider a relationship.

The bus circumvents Buckingham Palace grounds. He has been inside once or twice. He told Mandy about the garden parties and his aristocratic background had enthralled her. Mandy originally was from Croydon, which Michael thought best not to mention to his mother. When they met he said she was from the county of Surrey. The summer has been good to him. His family have two shows running in London. One has the family money invested and in the other, he spends large amounts of Francine's wealth. So far, there is a working loss on this production totalling four million pounds, and still they spend, as if there is no end to the funding.

The bus reaches Hyde Park Corner and turns through to Piccadilly. Michael is planning another show and there could be a place for Mandy. He made this investment while scouting around Edinburgh's fringe festival. The production is a tribute to the girl pop trios and still playing to good houses. It would be a little brutal, but he could remove any one of the three leads and Mandy could step into any of the shoes, such is her professional ability. To Michael, this was one of her attractive qualities, she is totally reliable and he admires anyone who never disappoints in work and love. When he does finally find someone to share his life and fortune, he will be careful that they never disappoint him, or his family. His mind wanders again to the French musical and the promise that has yet to be fulfilled. The production has been a catalogue of waste and therefore it is frustrating to his meticulous mind. Now the French Producers have hired this girl, a girl called 'Tracie'. A 'Tracie' who has never appeared on a West End stage, whom they met while she was waiting their tables in a Criterion café bar! It could be the end of the show if she is too awful. Yet Julian and Francine believe it will be the beginning of a new era for their musical and the launch of a career for this talented, if a little unpredictable, teenager.

Up Piccadilly he jumps off the bus close to Fortnum and Mason. The entrance to The Fountain Room is in Jermyn Street and Michael cuts through the store to meet Mandy at the café's entrance. Mandy is on time, strolling towards him as if she is taking the stage on cue. Her hair is tied up and she has the Audrey Hepburn look about her today. They touch cheeks, kissing the air in greeting, and he smells her perfume. Michael would dearly love to lift up her dress, drop his own suit trousers and ravish her, but he has a thousand years of English reserve holding the jewels for another coronation. Instead he smiles gently, escorting her through the gilt swing doors and watching her swaying hips as they pass into the restaurant.

'I've booked for 1:30pm,' he says, looking at her luminous eyes sparkling at him. Taking their seats by the window, he ordered caviar and toast.

'Did they like it?' she asked. Michael looked quizzically at her, 'The tape! You said that you were going to show Julian and Francine the show tape!'

Michael held out the cassette, but before Michael could think of a way of breaking the news diplomatically she broached the subject.

'Seems a wasted effort filming it when they plan to replace me anyway,' she said nonchalantly,

Michael was stunned but privately relieved that she knew.

'This Tracie girl, yes, I've met her. I quite liked her really. Felt a bit sorry for her, I think she was high on drugs, and, well she told me everything, poor lamb.'

'Have you said anything to them?' he asked.' Do they know that you know?'

'Oh yes, they want me to teach her all the moves for my number in the show. I said I would, but they'll have to pay me extra, if they want her to get the right steps.'

Michael was shocked at her indifference. 'This doesn't bother you?'

Mandy took a scoop of caviar on her toast and looked Michael in the eye.

'My agent, signed a yearlong contract, remember? I'm bound to that contract for a year, so are Julian and Francine. Whether they fire me, or not they still have to pay me. There's a space coming up in 'Blood Brothers' this month, which my agent thinks I should get. If this 'Tracie' is as crap as I know she is, then they'll ask me back and if I am free, I shall consider it. If not I shall be in 'Blood Brothers' heading for Broadway. Either way it's Win, Win!'

They finished the meal and she insisted on paying her share. 'I know we have been close, Michael darling, and it has been fun, but as they say all good things must come to an end, and this must have been a good thing because it's over.'

She left Michael standing open-mouthed and walked to the door. As her hand touched the handle, she turned and spoke back at him. 'Oh, can I have the show tape?' she asked. Michael handed her the wrapped cassette. Mandy smiled at him raising the corner of her mouth, the mouth he dearly wanted to be his, before she let him go forever.

'You are a dear,' she said her nose touching his, 'I don't know how I'll ever manage without you.'

THE DRESSING

1983

The dresser waits with the soda salts ready to quench the turmoil of Alessandro's ulcerated stomach. He has suffered with internal pains ever since he arrived from Paris and believes it is the hard London waters that affect him. His face has a striking angularity. It is a face that usually projects emotions, but now does not reveal the pain and the battle inside him. Anita is for him the nurse and mother. She wonders if she is also a potential lover to the magician and yet their relationship is akin to that of servant and master. Anita shares his Portuguese heritage, and they speak often in their common language, when they wish to be private. They are two people with a similar language and this makes their relationship more compatible. Her family are not available to meddle in her life and his family have given up trying to make him conform. Alessandro's parents do not approve of him. He is, in their minds, a man-chasing degenerate who forsook the church, the saints and defiled the Papal ministry. When he tried to settle for the seminary in Brasilia, the combined forces of his community breathed a sigh of relief. For they thought this young man would now only have the potential to corrupt the Church and the mightiness of such an institution should be strong enough to resist. The family thanked their God that under such tutelage of the priesthood, Alessandro would not stray into the dark waters of sin. As the embrace of a God washes the sins, so would the child, by his association with others learn not drown in such sins? Alessandro learned not only to paddle, but swim beyond the depths of depravity. At the seminary he met others who questioned the validity of the organisation and together they openly flaunted its rules for their enjoyment. When he was de-frocked and returned to the community, who had so proudly projected him to sainthood, he was as unwelcome as a fart in a confessional box. This brush with costume, however, did find him another area of pleasure, and he soon swapped the dark robes of a priest for more colourful vestments. He began to experiment with female impersonation and found employment in a club in the centre of Rio. It was a course that he continues to this day.

Anita loves his clothes. She has developed them from the clumsy characters they have been in all his other shows, to technically efficient machines, of which she has control. Anita sits among the festooned clothing and listens to Alessandro retch. The fizzling cocktail of Andrews salts in her hand calms the glass, but does little to help with his acid attack. Anita's family are from Portugal and migrated to South Africa, settling in the white suburbs. This is what it says on her South African passport. She once found love with and English girl and she married that love, obtaining a precious passport. The marriage, attended by the family, only lasted a year and it is now over. Anita has a face that some would say is older, with deep furrows of natural worry tanned by the climate of her birth and shaped by the Latin culture of her parents. She left her home to become accepted and will one day return home again to try for that acceptance.

There is the sound of a flush in the cubicle and the door opens. Alessandro's hand reaches out and she places the glass into it. His hand retreats with the solution and Alessandro drinks, is sick and then can be heard drinking from the tap. When he finally emerges, he has the face of a boy that is slipping through the ages of man. He can have the look of a child, a woman, or who-ever he paints upon the canvas that is his face. As himself he is pallid and chipped by the acne that he has never lost. He reaches out and takes another full glass of mineral water presented to him by his dresser; he smiles a bleak expression showing his yellowing, aged teeth.

'Tomorrow we'll see a doctor,' she announces and he nods, resigned to the physical pain and her advice.

His clothes are laid out in the reverse order of the sequence they appear. His act is based on revelation and substitution of the characters he plays and his changes rely on the cloth that surrounds him. Alessandro's clothes make his new shape and in this new shape he becomes the characters, without the cloth he is a plain man. His face features a traditionally painted white mask as a clown's base. His character lines are accentuated by pencil line. Up close the make-up is grotesque, but to the auditorium, he is a God of beauty. He starts to dress, a base layer wraps around his middle cupping the elongated trunk, which he is careful to show only occasionally. Strands of hair peek around this cup that cuts hard into his groin, but he likes this compared to the sharp pains internally. A vest pushes at his thin frame, shaping his muscles to match the outer clothing. There are stockings that line his legs. He has a strong physique, but this stacked upon weak legs.

Anita takes the glass from him, so that he does not spill the water on his clothing. She is ready to proceed with his dressing ritual. A shirt straddles his chest and its silken coldness clings to the cotton undershirt. Anita smoothes the lines of the seams and her professional eyes see the areas, which he will show to the audience. Alessandro only has to elevate his arms and the garment becomes him. The anger in his belly is now forgotten. Over the base clothing is a top layer that folds to his shape, enhancing him, giving it colour and making him feel as secure as he did in his days as a priest. The blackness of his previous life has now left him and he is no longer a Jesuit. He sees himself and recognises with pleasure the full-length mirror bowing back at him. Anita blesses him as he takes the shape we now recognise from the show's advertisements.

The image is everything. A two dimensional character dressed in a black dress suit and a pocketful of magic. Anita wears what she needs, her clothing functional, her wristband is not decoration but a pad of pins for securing repairs to Alessandro's dress. Jeans contain and protect her against the ravages of London. Her breasts are heavy and sometimes painful, lifted by cups beneath a patterned chemise painted with delicate flowers on the printed light cotton. Her hair, raven in origin is now greying at the roots. She has it tied up and this prevents it getting in the way of her work. Alessandro beckons for water and receives a full glass, filled with the Italian spring water he thinks is shipped specially in for him. Anita has found his favourite brand on sale in Shaftsbury Avenue, to her water is water still tastes fine, even from a tap. He reaches across to the dressing table and takes a pillbox from a drawer. In a practised move, he puts a blue tablet to his tongue. The floodgates from the drug open and he feels stronger.

They talk to each other in Portuguese as if to try and ignore the country they are visiting. Each finds release in their language. For Anita it is the voice of her childhood, the language of her parents. She had two voices, Portuguese the language she used at home to rebel and spit fire, her twisted grammar handed down together with the accent from her parents; and the bastardised English that she speaks openly, her accent revealing the Africana English of her birth. Alessandro speaks in a cultured Rio dialect that denotes his education, His English is mannered but weak and he stumbles outside his true voice, always asking to be corrected to improve his vocabulary.

Alessandro has been using these pills for many weeks to enhance the pace of his living. The drug makes him fidget, but the long-term effects do not concern him. Anita prefers marijuana as her way to escape. She needs it to sleep and then to wake and smokes to follow each meal. She mainly needs the drug to help with the pain she finds has followed her after the surgery. She smokes cigarettes almost as much as she breathes and this lighted relief is interspersed with the crumbled natural drug she mixes with the tobacco. She is now finished and takes a break. This is the point when her fingers are anxious to be doing something else. When she is working, the cloth is stainless and pure. Anita is a surgeon to the stitching and washes her hands of any trace of tar before resuming her work.

The first costume has been assembled. Alessandro stands admiring himself in the mirror chasing each line to follow the eye that others will watch. If it were not Alessandro in the mirror, he would love the image and could weep at the beauty that other hands have created for him. The dresser is not just the servant to the performer. She is his caddy in more functions than is printed in the union contract.

'But we shall not become lovers!' he has said many times, in case Anita had not understood his accent.

Anita has to understand, construct and maintain each particle of clothing and engineer it to perform alongside its owner. She repairs, washes and replenishes the torn excesses of the show so that the 'Artiste', as the performers insist on being called, can function in front of the audience without worry that their fly zipper might open accidentally. There is a wardrobe department with a team of staff who are employed to maintain the costumes on an assembly line for the whole company. Today it might be a spangle bra that has become too tight and in need of an extra popper or Gerard's gusset that needs strengthening so that he can manage the high kicks. Anita was recruited as personal seamstress for her language skills secure her a place as Alessandro's personal costumier. Each star artiste has their own aide to help with the multiple changes and Alessandro's needs were more than most. Those who attend to the chorus serve the many and there is a distance between the departments. There is no closeness to their charges and the chorus dressers are the first to receive the sharp excess of adrenalin pumped anger, from a dancer who has struggled with a clothing malfunction. Anita has a respect from her 'Artiste', as he cannot be the performer without her constant attention. Alessandro dresses slowly and the next layer of the act is positioned across the first, changing his shape or colour, as the scene dictates. Alessandro likes Anita. She has a difference that he has not yet fathomed, and this intrigues him. In Paris he had a dresser he thought a clumsy child who was a mediocre seamstress and not much help, although she could service his other needs. She took more time over his dressing, but did not care for his clothing or the end result. Despite this they became lovers. This dresser knew that she had to share her man and was happy to join his ménage. Although a pleasing lover, she was not discreet and this upset Francine and he was not encouraged to employ her when the trip to London was offered. The Parisian dresser made a scene when she was told and made many allegations against her employer. Francine and Julian negotiated a settlement and consequently she received a sum of money that helped her find other employment. Alessandro is careful now that he does not cross that line with his staff, a line that separates him and possible union action against him. Alessandro still has an appetite for the female body and it is Francine who is his main outlet. His love of the female form equals that of his love of man. His earliest sexual thoughts stemmed from being pressed to a matronly breast within his home. In those breasts he found the smells, the silken black dress material and the sharpness of the lace provocative. Later in his childhood he changed his preference and became aroused when he saw a priest, he often wonders if it was the black material that attracted him. This effect crystallised when he was taken aside by one of the celibates for a measurement of his vestments, and was touched by the hand of Gods own before becoming an altar boy. It was not this experience that made him yearn for male company. The priest would vouch to his many cardinals that it was the devils own child who initiated the contact. Contact like this with another being was a serious confusion for the young boy, who did not know whether he preferred either barred sex. Alessandro was not ashamed of his desires and had a role model to legitimize these feelings. He had been a distant uncle, who Alessandro remembered, visiting the family home. The family told stories about Uncle Max being a one-time soldier of fortune, fighting in some South American republic, when he was not visiting his Brazilian cousins. Max was, by the time Alessandro reached 15, himself in his late fifties. He had, at one time, lived in the Northern U.S.A and then for sometime was the companion of a famous writer, who lived outside Santiago. While spying on his uncle in the shower Alessandro noticed he had a number tattooed on his arm, and on his back a triangle cut into his shoulder. The uncle always arrived from his travels and presented the younger members of the family with a show of magic. Max could produce coins, cards, sweets and even the odd rabbit, which was always taken and used in the pot for a later meal. Alessandro eagerly awaited these visits and would monopolize his uncle's time, learning the many techniques for distracting the audience's eye and creating the illusion of magic. Uncle Max showed Alessandro simple coin tricks such as the 'French drop' and the 'Misers Palm' and the boy practised these tricks, until his dexterity equalled the nimbleness of his mentor's fingers. Coins would vanish and appear, inappropriately passing through time and space between them. When Max left to join his friends elsewhere, Alessandro would practise these illusions and devour the books and cuttings from the theatrical papers, describing the new illusionists and their recent feats of deceit. Alessandro knew that what he studied was illusion and that there was no real magic involved. But he loved to make others believe that magic was 'real' and, since the world around him believed in the magic of the church, so they could be convinced, by a little trickery, that Alessandro also had magical powers. When Alessandro strayed into magic, his understanding was at odds with the church and this became an issue with parents. Hidden from the family, he took to quietly secreting himself in basements to study the blasphemy and learn the trade of illusions. His abilities were practiced by the hours he spent in study and he believed he was a Superman who could beat physics. Through magic, he found that he could go be beyond the human capabilities and this was a source of pleasure for him. Of all the illusions that he had read about in his studies of magic, flight was the one thing he most wished to achieve. There was a medieval illusionist who could hypnotise audiences en masse and make them believe the magician was leaving the ground by unnatural means. This was Alessandro's ambition and it is only in his adulthood that Alessandro managed with the art of his illusions to fly. He always thanks his Uncle Max for launching him when he lifts from the ground in his favourite illusion.

Anita watches him as his hands twist and conceal the silver disc he plies through his fingers. Alessandro repeats this ritual before each performance, and is always thinking about his tutor. Anita puffs on her cigarette and the smoke fills her chest, before expiring into the small window that leads out into the air well. This is an old theatre and each of the internal dressing rooms has an air vent that allows the number of dressing rooms to each have a window. These vents provide light and air to the performers who need the natural cooling elements while getting dressed for the show. The smoke rising from Anita's cigarette trickles up this air well and disturbs pigeons, which call down to her from their precarious nests in annoyance. It is nearing the half hour call. Most of the performers have been in for the past hour, are dressed, and have made up their faces and limbered for the performance. Alessandro has spent most of the afternoon inside his dressing room fingering the fabrics on the hangers and talking to Anita, while she stitches, smokes and reads magazines. Everyone concerned with the performance has to be present thirty-five minutes before a show otherwise the understudies, or 'swing' will be put on standby and have to be paid for the performance. The thirty-minute call is in fact thirty-five minutes, as there is always a five-minute hiatus on stage before the curtain goes up. The clock is ticking, punctuated by the Tannoy calls from the stage manager announcing the time. Alessandro uses this time to meditate while Anita fusses around his costume. He believes this ritual has to be observed, lest his skills desert him in the performance. During the day he needs others around him and either Anita or one of his current acolytes will usually join him to share lip-glosses and the latest gossip, but this time is for his private preparation and he appears distant to the other performers. Anita smokes to the end of the Dunhill and stubs out the expensive gold ringed filter, extinguishing the flame and burning her index finger. She is wondering about the prop boy and how to end all association, as the affair has not been one of her better choices.

'What are you thinking about?'

'The boy',

'He's listening outside the door. He often does that.'

Anita gets up and goes to the door. She pulls it open quickly, expecting to find the props boy with ear poised to the lock. There is no one outside the dressing room and she turns to see Alessandro laughing at her distress. The prop boy has escaped, running upstairs to give the cast notes from the management. Anita has not been able to talk to the boy since her revelation to him and she is angry that his statement of love for her is compromised by her previous gender. Anita returns to her seat and lights up another Dunhill. She smokes with anger, she smokes with food and she smokes while waiting for food. She will even smoke while waiting for another cigarette. Her lungs and skin have hardened to the nicotine and tar, eating into her lung space. The smoke curls around her head weaving patterns around her prematurely greying hair. The strands of grey mingle with to the trails of evaporating soot, swirling around her face. Her hair is still long and she ties it up to accentuate her neck and shoulders, one of the things that made the youth fall in love with her. The cigarette touches her angular lips. The boy admired her lips, the freckles and collection of moles that had chosen her face and created her beauty. She has lost him now and was sure his love was juvenile and skin deep. Within the confines of the thirty-minute call the theatre is coming alive, anticipation growing of the performance ahead. It is a countdown that has no way of stopping until the curtain lifts, when the collective adrenalin starts pumping through the company. There are two hundred people working in the building this night, and each of them feel the clock ticking to an unstoppable launch.

This production is a pyramid of performers and technicians, who create the entertainment and at the pinnacle of the structure, is the magician. There is no understudy to Alessandro. It was suggested by Michael Leighton to assign a cover, and then the idea was retracted as it offended Francine, who treasured Alessandro's very individual contribution. She said that Alessandro is a one-off and although it is thought that he is grooming the Headwaiter to be his English successor should he leave, he has no heir apparent. Behind the dressing room door, Alessandro has taken refuge in his cubical where, on the thirty-minute call, he realises that he is contractually obliged to perform to this London audience and he becomes afraid of the responsibility.

Anita, having already spent ten hours in the building closes her eyes and rests for her preparatory tasks are done. She too has to prepare for performance, as she will be as busy as the performers, managing Alessandro's quick changes. The Dunhill wedged between her fingers hangs loosely below her while she drifts off. She rarely sleeps for long and such napping is commonplace. Yesterday had been a long night for, after finishing the show she and Alessandro spent another few hours in the bar mixing with the audience, before leaving to dance at another club in Soho. When Anita returned to her home in the early hours, she did not undress but changed her shoes and tied back her hair with a new band, before leaving to catch the bus back into town. She uses the number 23 bus, from her home to the theatre passing from Holland Park through Ladbroke Grove and Notting Hill before arriving in the West End at Marble Arch. Invariably she sleeps on the bus between stops, as the undulations hypnotise her in conjunction with the diesel engine that growls through each gear. She dreams of many things, often her dreams are about South Africa and her family, to whom she would like to return. The upper deck still allows smoking and if she stays awake, she will have at least one of her Dunhill's before they reach Oxford Street, and a further two on the walk through Soho to the Regent Theatre. There is always a list of repairs from the previous performance and she religiously commits these jobs to a notebook as a reminder. From 8:30 am she works in the dressing room washing, cutting and mending the magicians clothing so they are perfect for the performance. She had a short spell of private life with the boy and managed both work and love. That was then. Those are just dreams and over. Anita lifts the cigarette to her lips, instinctively knowing where she is and what she was doing before she drifted off.

'Fifteen minutes, Ladies and Gentlemen. Fifteen minutes. Thank You'

The theatre community steps up its activity and there is a growing urgency that emanates from the building as the Tannoy announces the audience is being let into the auditorium. Potentially there is a thousand punters, sitting down to a meal and a show having paid fifty pounds each.

'Alessandro, it's time to get dressed. Hurry up you lazy shit!'

There is no sound from within the toilet. This is not unknown; he sometimes uses this moment to sleep. But this time there is no sound. Anita calls to him through the panelled wood frame and there is no answer to her calling. She knows this is not like him. Anita pushes at the door and sees Alessandro poised haphazardly on the toilet. The spirit appears to have left him and there is no sound of breathing. She lunges towards him and as soon as her hands make contact with his body he takes a breath inwards. This death rattle is a shock to Anita and she steps back as his piercing blue eyes opening from within his skull, staring her full in the face. The clothing that she has carefully crafted, hangs by his ankles and he is dribbling from the corner of his mouth, without realising it.

'Fuck, I've just ironed those.'

Alessandro remembers who he is. Anita retreats to her sofa and lights another cigarette to let him complete his toilet and dress. She waits for five minutes, until the cigarette has dropped all its goodness into the ashtray. Alessandro emerges and without looking at her in his embarrassment. He sits at his table of lights and finishes the lines of his make up, straightening any blemish with another layer of plaster.

'Sorry'.

'No more pills!'

'No more pills.'

He powders his face and breathes in the mixture of dust and tobacco that has begun to cloud his table. He gets up and runs back to the cubicle, wrenching his stomach that now only contains water and the blue pills he had taken to keep himself awake. Anita has little sympathy for him and waits for him to finish before calling his name sharply.

'Alessandro'

There is silence and a rhythmical banging on the door to his toilet. She drops the remaining filter into the ashtray and jumps up from her chair. The door to the toilet is blocked and she struggles to release the dead weight of Alessandro behind it. The sound is his arms flailing in a seizure against the wood panelling. His eyes open and rolling, his mouth oozing bubbles of white churned phlegm, reminiscent of cappuccino froth. She reaches to him and he stabilises, then wakes, scared, for he has travelled through a hell alone in those few seconds and can only remember instances in his pain. The inside of his mouth turns red and he spits out the damage, as he has bitten his tongue. The white spittle now runs crimson across his powdered white face, distorting his image to that of a second rate Dracula.

'Ladies and Gentlemen this is your five minute call. Five minutes, please!'

Anita picks his dead weight up from the floor and pulls him through to the room. She nurses his head wiping the blood and fluids from his mouth. He is sick and covers the costume with a watery blanket. Anita holds him and does not flinch from the mess. He wakes and is comforted by her hand on his brow. Louder voices emanate through the Tannoy from the auditorium, as the house fills up, an audience expecting a performance to a standard. Alessandro rises from the floor and sits himself at his table. Anita follows him with a wetted cloth and cleans the patch of vomit from his costume, until it regains its original splendour. Alessandro cannot speak since his tongue is too swollen, so it is then fortunate that his act is in mime. He shakes and rushes back to the cubicle in an explosion of quivering projection. The door slams and he plasters the basin.

'Ladies and Gentlemen, This is your beginner's call. Gentlemen of the orchestra, stage management and dressers to the stage please. Mr Maenza and all members of the cast to the stage for the opening number, Thank you.'

Still there is little word from the toilet.

FALL OF THE DANCER'S CAREER

2006

Ellen relives the fall, before the fall and the life after the fall. In going back she holds the memory of her time with mobility, Poised and able. It is only now because she is fixed at navel level that she can remember the difference. It is the same memory we all have in growing from childhood to adulthood but in reverse. When we are children we look up to everyone physically. The hem of the skirt, the belt buckle, these are our eye line. Adults have to bend down to us to converse and we are constantly reminded that our true place in society will be when we are standing ten feet tall amongst our fellows. Ellen has been tall, her place in society earned and her ability to stand on her points lifted her higher than most of her peers. Since the fall she has reverted to the height of a child forever confined to a sitting position. She is physically placed below society watching even her son grow tall and adult beside her. The pain, for there was pain in that moment, this is now forgotten, superseded by new senses of emptiness. Pain is relative to areas that can feel and much of her body does not have that feeling. The fall saw the receptors switched to the off position. Maybe in a future therapy those receptors will be activated again, maybe, but not perhaps in her lifetime, for she has limits now. It was a clumsy stupid mistake. There were too many people in too small a space and the result was predictable. The corridors designed to house one person at a time for an entrance to the stage and not designed for a collection of manic chorus girls in heels.

There are protocols in the theatre some are the myth and some legend, others a link to a historical fact and others that are plain common sense. When an uninitiated young actor whistles within the walls of a theatre, he does so without the knowledge that he could be signalling the movement of scenery. The training in theatre arts includes these myths as part of the safety instructions. Often the history of these myths is unknown. We do not whistle anymore to our colleagues above the stage, for there are telecommunications that give more direct information. Yet we still adhere to these traditions. Ascending and descending stairs is another of these 'do not' measures, yet in reality this is just common sense. When the Victorians designed their theatres they did so with a limitation of space that in today would have not been sanctioned. Old style dressing rooms are small and stuffy and toilets and showers basic; stairwells are tight and sheer. The first rule one learns is that no person should pass another on the stairs. This potential superstition had more to do with the restricted access than the irrational fears of those within the building. When four of the chorus girls left the dressing room together on that evening, they did so because each realised that they were late for their cue. Over the run of the production they had begun to build an audio picture of the show from the crackly Tannoy speaker above the door. When the sound of a certain tune or speech reached the upstairs, they left their make up, and dressed in their next presentation, heading downwards to the stage level.

The longer the run of the production, the more time the girls gave themselves before starting the descent. On this occasion they had overstepped their allowance of time and as a flock realised that they were going to miss the entrance to the Venice scene. In the clatter to get from the 5th floor to the stage level, they collectively forgot the golden rule. This truth combined with gravity caused the accident. As in every accident, there is usually damage. It was Ellen who was damaged.

She woke to find herself in an awkward position. Even for a dancer who can contort into many unusual shapes, this position was unnatural. She was unable to focus visually and in hindsight this was a blessing for it saved her the extra pain of seeing where she had landed. The girls around her were quickly ushered onto the stage and within a beat of music stepped into their characters, all be it one less. The stage manager and one other company member held Ellen's hand and felt her paled brow. In one lucid moment Ellen saw the blue eyes of a man looking at her. His sockets were sparkled and the eyebrows painted. The colours in his eyes pulled her towards his face and she swam with him in her deluded state. Charles held her hand and watched this swan seeping life away from him. She had the demeanour of road-kill limping across the carriageway, before the arrival of another lorry. His white linen suit became stained from the grime of the floor and the blood stains of the girls injured body. His precision penned eye make up streaked, as he thought he saw Ellen slip away from him, reminding him of his Mother when she let go of his hand as she died.

Separated by the stage manager from his charge, Charles was propelled on to the front stage to resume his duties, while Ellen, was then taken away by the paramedics. When she woke after the operation Ellen said that she remembers an 'angel', at her side. He had a white suit and painted eyes and smelt of the kitchen.

THE PROPS BOY
HALF HOUR CALL

1983

He is taking the choreographer's notes around to the dressing rooms. It is one of the things that he does. He delivers other people's messages and checks that everyone has what they want. He has to put on his own costume before the half hour call and changing in the stage management office is not his choice. He is technically not in the cast. There is no electrically lit mirror, nor a place for the props boy to add his make up. He does not wear any powder, as it has never been suggested it matters that his face needs to be seen. The props boy is only a body, a technician that walks the stage occasionally and yes, he does serve Alessandro's act and even earned a small part in the Venice scene, but these forays on to the stage do not make him a performer. As if to remind him of his true status, he visits each dressing room to make sure that the each of company have arrived and deliver any messages from the management. Beginning at the men's dressing room at the top of the stairwell he works downwards, letting gravity guide his commission. For the male dancers, the timekeeper is never popular and the requests from the management are not welcome. The management think the choreography has become slack and the tambourine number will be cut if the performers do not shape up their presentation. The boy knows this fact, as he has secretly read the typed words that constitute an official warning to the male chorus. The men are confined into one dressing room, airless and dank. Posters of previous shows in this theatre adorn the walls, bleached out by the years of high wattage light bulbs, which fire definition onto the mirrors and rouged faces. Camp exchanges are common, the more vulgar the better. Howls of pleasure greet the knock and when the door opens the volume increases as the boy joins them.

Male dancers are not given the credit for their magnificence, they are the human cranes to the glamorous girls and in only one number do they dance with the skill that is their gift. These men's various sexual tastes are not hidden in the dressing room and the occupants have no need to hide their preferences from each other. They dress, as do their female counterparts, in glitz rather than practical solutions, underpinned by the pouches that keep their manhood in position.

'Come in' one queen cries from behind the white painted oak door and the boy enters the room and smiles tentatively.

'Half hour gentlemen.' and they all chorus 'Thank you.'

The faces of the men are being applied with garish make-up, which is their preparation for the opening number. Followed by the clean muscular bodies in thin Lycra underwear, they absorb other features. The props boy hovers a moment watching them dress.

'And?' says Joel his eyebrows arched. The boy hands over the note and waits for a reply. 'Then fuck off boy, unless you want something.'

He shakes his head and leaves them to discuss what they could offer a nineteen-year old props boy. He skips down the stairwell and reaches another door, knocks with less confidence and waits for the command to enter.

'Come in.' shout a chorus of high pitched female voices. Taking a deep breath he turns the dirty brass handle, gripping the lever with expectation.

To be welcomed here is where his pleasure begins. Seeing twenty beautiful, and sometimes, near naked young women is never a chore and something that he shall not forget. They all squeal as the 'pet' joins their quickly covered bodies. Boas are thrown across his neck, kisses planted onto him and powder is sprinkled onto his face, which help to diffuse the sights of breasts travelling from street to stage brassieres.

'I have a note from the Choreographer,' he splutters and Suzanne, taking the typed communication from him, tweaks his bum. 'If I don't like what I read, you are going to be . . . !' She never finishes her sentence and he nods, knowing that this would never happen.

As they pass the note around the boy waits, watching like a sponge to amass a repertoire of images that he can call upon later.

Each of the girls in the chorus has a different costume and a label that denotes who wears it. These outfits cling on rows of hangers in the dressing room and secretly he wishes that he could hang amongst them.

Chairs are lined up in front of the mirrors opposite the costumes so that the girls can put on their make-up and select their first frock without getting in each other's way. When the girls are painting themselves, they all look the same. The base of pancake is a simple mask that flattens the face, on which with the artistry of detail portrays perfect womanhood.

There are ten in the chorus dressing room, conveniently positioned next to the wardrobe department, so that the bulk of the washing and mending need not travel far. The girls only appear together in the finale of the show and spend most of the night divided into small groups, performing while the rest are changing for the next number. None seem to realise the boy is standing with them. There is no reply to the note, although he should be shuffling away, he stands rigid by the half open door and hoping to fade into the mist.

At the first seat is Ellen, she has been dancing for many years with the Irish National Ballet and has earned her place in the company for her experience. As a child she was an Irish dancer until, when as a teenager, she was taken by the ballet and projected into the Irish National stage where her professional life was mapped out. She is soon to retire and this production will be her swansong. She looks up at the boy and smiles as he looks down to avoid her gaze.

Suzanne sits next to her. She is South African, with Dutch heritage, and is travelling with her companion. She has stopped in Europe to make a little money and London is her latest home. She has a biker boyfriend, who arrives each day with her perched on his motorcycle. Her face is pot marked by acne, which she tries to ignore but glares at her each time she passes a mirror. Her body is formidable, which is the focus of the audience when she is revealed in a semi-nude costume and they do not register the face behind the make-up. She has read the choreographer's note and plans to ignore the recommendations.

Joy is, as her name would suggest, young and naïve, but has a pleasant demeanour. She will toughen up during the rehearsals and, if tough enough, she will stay. She has, by her lack of experience to try harder than the others to keep in the chorus. The boy would like more than anything to see her naked, for she, unlike the other girls in the chorus has never shown her full body to an audience and this secrecy is her allure. The boy looks at her back and she ignores him, for she is focused on her eyeliner and as a consequence, he does not exist.

Jenny does not want anyone to know that she works here. She will not work as a Cabaret dancer for long, as she has plans to change her name and try for the Ballet in San Francisco. With legs, curled under the table they extend in one through line to her shoulders, or so men like to think. The boy's attention fixes on her feet as the note is passed to her and she sniggers and passes it on. She does not care for the criticism as she is only working here until her visa arrives. This Cabaret has little value to her but for now will make her a living.

In the third seat sits Mandy. 'Dancer and Singer' it says on her C.V. Mandy has played pantomime for the past ten years. The props boy has known of her because her mother's dance school is near to his parent's home. Her singing voice sends goose bumps up his neck and she has an educated plum speaking voice that has cost her mother much money and her many hours of practise.

'Has anyone seen my tiara?'

'Where you left it Duchess,' calls one of her fellows.

Mandy used to have a dressing room of her own when she was a featured singer but now has handed it over to Tracie, who is currently 'jacking up' in her own private toilet. Mandy has no regrets at her demotion, for she has already accepted a contract to join the new musical 'Blood Brother's'. The prop boy's hand touches the door handle and he looks to the end seat to see in the reflected wall, a young fawn dabbing her eyes with a tissue.

Her boyfriend has hurt Terri again, or maybe she has some mascara caught in her eyelid, he doesn't stop to ask. Terri will always be looking for a man with a loving nature to help her get over this unfortunate experience. She loves cooking and has a cat called Theo.

In the seat near to the sink is Janet. She is the sister of the current 1500 metre Olympic champion and has only managed to keep this fact secret because she knows that the publicity of her nightly public nudity might harm her brother's ambitions. He is very proud of her, but is also careful not to broadcast the connection, in case it affects his chances of a political career.

Denny has always wanted to be in a West End show and has achieved her ambition to make it as the understudy to the chorus. Being the 'swing' is like being the substitute in a football match, with little chance of a full game. She knows that any casualty could result in her playing in any position. She has been told that she is a little overweight for the costumes and feels intimidated by the other girls and their constant diets. To maintain a shape desired of the management's wishes, she is in a constant extreme of binge and starvation. If her size stands out in the line she will be replaced, so she regularly vomits a good meal to keep her job.

The chorus have been working hard for the past three weeks, every day in extra rehearsal and each night, to entertain the audiences. Lingering, with his note for the girls dispatched the props boy feels that he should leave now and not become a voyeur absorbing their perfume. The reviews have been dreadful, but the audiences still come and the 'houses' appear to be full most nights, even though they are heavily papered with complimentary tickets. The girls have been rehearsing a new number today with Alessandro and the director. There was excitement when Jean-Paul arrived and most in the company feel he has improved the production. There have been some additions, such as the 'Dinosaur Women', for example. The girls cringe when the music begins for they have to run around in little fur bikinis, holding spears and chanting to an imaginary sun god, while the two dinosaurs fight to the death before shedding their skins, revealing two women simulating lesbian fucking, to the pulsing disco soundtrack by Aaron Copeland. All the company is convinced it is only the director and his wives who enjoy this segment of the show.

The chorus have been in the building two hours before the call. They joined in a class led by the dance captain, who drilled them in stretching routines. They had a meeting to assign the scenes before going to their rooms to make up and dress. The boy jumps down the stairwell in long bounds singing as he descends.

His job is done, the notes have been delivered and every member of the chorus accounted for. The Artistes' on the lower floors are dressed and ready, swapping dressing rooms and admiring each other in a psyching up of their pre-show nerves. The boy stops outside the dressing room of the French models and knocks. Claire is a name she tells to him was given to her by her agent, as her African name was difficult to pronounce. She opens the door and seeing the boy arches her head in mock deference.

'Hello there.' Her voice is soft and heavily accented. She only knows the English words of greeting and fornication, both of which seem universal. She is alone and invites him in with an open door and sway of her hand.

He walks into her lair, noticing that her dark body is completely naked. She touches his shoulder, closes the door, the note is delivered, and after a short time he is allowed to leave. Only Alessandro and Anita remain on the boy's itinerary. He hesitates at the door, for outside he can hear the words coming from within that he dare not meet. Alessandro's voice can be heard in a mocking tone say, 'he's outside, listening'. The boy runs back up the stairs away from their door, lest he is caught eves dropping.

There are a few minutes left before the beginners call. Up to the roof, re-tracing his steps, the boy runs past all the doorways until in seconds he reaches the night sky. It is his last duty before the show begins. Making his way across the moonlit terrace he goes to the aviary to select one of Alessandro's doves. There are now only four of the six purchased left living, two have already escaped. It was Alessandro who let them loose, when he was careless during their training and they flew off to assimilate into the life of the street pigeons. Alessandro showed the boy how to dock their tail feathers to stop them flying off and it is a job he dislikes, for they sometimes bleed and he feels their pain. The props boy's job is to tend these creatures and he spends much of his working week here, feeding and cleaning out their cages as part of his routine. On a hot day he will pretend to be working and really he is sitting on the flat tar the roof writing in a notebook. Entering their cage, he selects one dove for tonight's show. It flutters and fights until the boy has it tightly held, where it succumbs for him to either break its neck, or take it to the stage. The boy is aware of the power he has over this little creature and vows not to harm it.

THE SHOW REPORT

1983

Remembering to carefully lock the aviary and with his charge, he travels back to the stage level where he deposits, the now tranquil creature into it's small cage on the props table in time for the 'beginners' call. The Parade has all the individual acts displayed in a Greek chorus. It has the appearance more like a circus than a theatrical production. The boy takes his place alongside the stage manager at the prompt desk. She is a fashion mannequin dressed in cutting edge 80's street wear that she swears comes from her contacts at the nearby St Martin's Art School. She barely acknowledges the prop's boy and is never seen socially with him. The boy stands alongside her in a cheap costume, aware that it needs to be sent to the laundry. The desk contains an array of lights and switches red for a standby and a green for a go. Each department sits with a light awaiting their call, each electrical string co-ordinated by the puppet master at the prompt corner. On stage level are the props, scenery and crew, setting and repairing they work in tandem with the lights flashed to test bulbs and warm the dust from the lenses.

'Take your place' he is told by the Stage Manager and without quibble, he scuttles away to his first position to double check his props.

The artistes start to appear, the girls first, they are instinctively trained to warm themselves up with stretches, their nimble anorexic frames arch in the poses of Degas pictures. Behind them appear the male dancers, who join in with the girls assuming positions of support and poses to warm their strong frames. The opening number contains oversized double bass, drums and sax magnified to four times their natural size, which are inhabited by the dancers in the jazz medley. The men of this scene take their positions, shutting themselves into the darkness as the stage working lights dim to begin the performance. The stage manager in the black, blue light of the arena whispers, 'beginners go, house lights go, band go, and stand by tabs.' Anita walks past the boy, followed by Alessandro who passes behind her 'zombified' and smelling of vomit. The band prepare for the start. They have received a red light from the stage manager, a preparation for the first music cue.

In the front of house, the audience have been patiently sitting, listening to a selection of popular hits on the taped soundtrack, while being served by the waiting staff. Tickets have been issued in advance and in the foyer, yet still late arrivals wishing to purchase a table are filling into the shrinking auditorium as the band ends its musical overture. Once the green light is thrown, there is no stopping this 'animal'. The cue light releases a chain of happenings that dovetail one into another and each link pushes relentlessly to a conclusion in an hour's time. The band, receive the green light and start with the opening bars of their first tune, the curtain rises and the front of house and stage lights flood the stage with artificial light. Colours and shapes spangle back and mix with the taped applause that the director has woven into his vision. The dancers jive in time to the mimed lyrics, earnestly competing with each other across the void that is the stage edge. They pretend to know the audience individually and yet cannot see a single eye across the shield of tungsten light. The lights change on cue from the prompt corner. From above, scenery drops to the stage to join the vast instruments. These instruments move aside to the wings as if by the magic of stage shifters and we are into the second scene; a set of steps that flash when walked over by stiletto heel.

The music changes, a sedate build of melodic sound is heard as each of the models walk down the steps, parading the scenery, worn as a costume. The whole audience breathes as one, as they see nudity mixed with fashion. It is every woman's desire, to be them and every man's dream to touch them. How the passion surges when this beauty is paraded. The props boy hands a wand of glitter to Anita who passes it to Alessandro's quaking hand. All the artistes appear on the stage and a full chorus of sound rises to a crescendo as a lift descends from the heavens, holding a host of angels with Alessandro at its centre. The magician seems nervous and yet it is his place to dominate the skies. He descends attached to a safety line and the metal gantry. The boy puts out his hand to Anita touching the edge of her skin and she snaps it away from him. Alessandro steps from his cloud and the angels fly from the stage to the heavens, blowing their trumpets. He walks forward to the centre stage and is joined by the props boy who enters the light pushing a cage on wheels. Alessandro produces a red silken scarf from his sleeve and throws a bloody screen around the prop. There is a flash and the music changes. Alessandro and the boy look at each other, his gaze fixed outside the walls of the theatre, and mechanically sprinkles glitter dust over the cage. There is a flash of light and the boy disappears through a trap door to the under stage and hearing above, the applause as Alessandro pulls at the red silk and reveals a girl from out of thin air. She stands up from her confinement, snarling at the audience in a tiger costume, cut so high that her body declares its availability.

Music plays and under the stage the props boy scrambles back up the stairwell. Claire steps from her dressing room, passing the boy, without acknowledging that minutes before they were lovers. 'My names Do Do Do Do Dollar' sings the tiger girl over the intercom. Onstage, Alessandro holds out his hand and she steps forward. Alessandro walks upstage and delivers more sprinkles of magic, and then in a piercing light, slips under the stage unseen. The boy returns to his position alongside the stage manager, no longer a performer but obedient stage technician. In the limelight, the tiger girl stretches her hands out to the audience and from the roof of the theatre, dollar bills cascade to the tables. The audience reach up in delight as the money showers them. The waiters squeal and run around, pretending to find real money and encouraging the diners to collect the dollar notes around them. Some of the paper money falls onto the lights around the proscenium and it is the props boy's job to rescue any stray notes, lest they ignite on the powerful spot lamps.

When this song finishes, a tall dancer, dressed as a ringmaster walks onstage with a whip. He cracks the weapon expertly and the tiger girl turns to him and snarls. They circle each other, he pushing her towards the middle of the stage, where seven poles are set into the floor. There are silver stepped podiums with soft red velour cushions, on each where sits a beautiful girl pouting, and about to pounce. The dollar girl joins them and the circus master cracks the whip. The girls raise their legs to a perfect forty-five degree angle, rotating their bodies as they reveal their true species'. The Ringmaster cracks the whip and they turn to show their underside fur bent double looking seductively at the audience from a position of submission. The whip cracks four more times and each provocative stance calls for the girls to join the cage. He cracks the whip for a last time and the girls' rush the ringmaster, whose clothes fall from him. The tiger girls run to the poles and for the next three minutes, they cavort up and down the shiny poles. The props boy likes this part of the show and makes himself a nest in the metal gantry, where he has an uninterrupted view. Alessandro is at the side of the stage being sick into the wings. Anita holds his cloak away and the boy sees her tending to him with a tenderness she once gave him.

'Put this on', says Anita offering the clown suit. 'Is the harness too loose?' He says not. The stage crew connect him to the cherry picker imported from South Africa and pull on their black masks, which makes the operators disappear into the shadows. The boy climbs down from his perch and changes into his next costume in front of the stage manager. She flicks the switch and the green light shows on her desk. The music plays a circus theme, the lights dim throughout the theatre. Lights spot onto the doorway of what appears to be a circus tent, while a technician fills the stage with smoke from a smoke machine.

A circus entrance painted onto a single cloth descends and in front of this artifice, Alessandro walks forward as a Pierrot clown. He looks to either side of the stage and gently levitates from the stage floor and slowly starting to revolve until he is upside down in the doorway. The music changes and the doorways of the tent fly upwards. Alessandro sheds his clown costume, as his feet return to the ground. Standing in an empty stage, in a black dress suit he clicks his fingers and from a podium a voice is heard. Mandy sings in a spotlight. Below her the band accompanying her melodic voice modulating in time to his movements as Alessandro lifts from the stage. Alessandro travels upwards as if on wires. His arms undulate towards the audience in wave patterns that take them with him in spirit. It is why they are here. The performers are the purveyors of this artifice and the props boy, with Alessandro share his triumph. Ronnie is also living a dream. It is he, whose home is an open door each Sunday, where he shares his music with friends who, for their part drink his wine and share his vision. Alessandro soars, as does the music and he climbs to the roof of the theatre, sweeping over the audience without wires. When he returns, there is a commotion as the audience melt in their applause, rich, loving applause that showers the Magician. He has defied gravity and flown, and the illusion of flight is conquered. Mandy, although she is counting the days until she leaves the production feels anointed. She sings an interlude at the front of the stage, a version of the classic jazz hit 'Running Wild'. Tracie joins her for the chorus, and they harmonise for the second and third verse. Soon it will be Tracie on her own singing this number. The front cloth descends from the extended roof of the stage.

Unseen technicians above haul ropes of counterbalanced and weighted structures, sweating and yet silently the men exert their skill and precisely touching the new setting to the stage. The flying machine and Alessandro have been disconnected and an 'all clear' is given to the stage manager. Another green light is directed to the band who, start to play 'the Venice theme'. Green gauze foliage falls into the stage from the roof, a controlled decent tethered to scaffold bars. Statues are set in poetic poses and the lighting undulates in a turquoise pattern. Amongst the statues are semi-clothed dancers and hidden in the half-light, their silhouettes hide their real, breathing bodies. The boy stands alongside Hugo and the two black models, one of who contains his scent. They hold wooden torches at arms length, frozen statues in a subterranean lagoon. A thin ballerina dances out to a tape of Neil Diamond singing a ballad. The tune calls for slow, measured steps, which she executes perfectly. The boy feels the warmth of the light on his bleached face. Hugo grins maniacally drawing the crowd to his position. The props boy sneaks a look to Claire and she signals to him a token of her affection. Jenny, who trained with the Royal Ballet School, dances a two-minute spot in which to show her skills. She stands, poised on one leg with her other vertically raised, effortlessly controlling muscles that we, ordinary mortals would never use. Alongside the two models, another prima ballerina comes alive and dances from the plinths to the centre stage. It is not the usual dancer, for Ellen on her way down from the dressing room has tripped in the stairwell. Denny was behind her on the stairs and says she saw everything. It was the heel of her shoe that gave way and Denny says that despite her trying to grab at Ellen, she fell and continued to fall down the thirty steps. Denny, like the trooper she is, went on in her place smiling, as if nothing had happened. Hugo and the boy, clumsily parade themselves beside the two beauties, watching them remove their clothing and baring their breasts to the soloist, in an offering of their fertility and availability. At this climax, the gauze behind floods with light upstage to reveal Alessandro and his props table. He is dressed in a silver studded jacket and a Mozart wig. He produces doves from his hands and juggles a magic ball through the air, floating with it and playing catch around the dancers all of them having now returned to their frozen state.

At the end of the act there is a crack of thunder and the stage visibly starts to shake. The audience gasp as they witness the demolition of Venice. Crashing live music pulsates from the band absorbing the voice of Neil Diamond from the tape. Scenery falls on cue to plotted locations, and as Venice disintegrates, it evolves into the backdrop of a pre-civilised history. Denny and Terrie appear at the back of the red sun cloth, shapely Neanderthal women screeching as they fight with their blunted spears. Downstage other dancers reel around each other and negotiate around the pop up scenery, as flash pots explode around them. There are lightning bursts and what once appeared to be rocks begin to morph into the shapes of huge lizards that turn to face each other. The leopard-skinned dancers leave the stage as the two lizards fight to the death. In a final death chord, the costumes split and from inside the leather suits appear two leathery naked women, their natural tans similar toned to the dinosaurs around them make love to each other in front of the audience, a display of a lesbian fantasy, intended to stimulate, yet shocking by its very candour. Mercifully the front cloth comes in quickly, the music changes to a comic patter and the show is catapulted into another direction.

A manic figure walks across the stage. He is a parody of an impressionist painter and pulls a paint frame on wheels eight foot high surrounded by a gilt frame. The figure lifts its mask to reveal it is Alessandro then he drops the mask again, to resume the characterisation. Alessandro skirts around the frame, switching position from the crouching props boy identically dressed as a painter and hiding from the audience view. The boy stands forward assuming the character left by Alessandro who is himself now hiding and changing costume. The new painter picks up a pot of paint, looks at the frame and then starts to paint the figure of Alessandro in the pose of the poster. As the painted figure is complete the eyes light up and the painter mimes a scream before disappearing down a smoke filled trap door. The props boy changes out of his costume under the stage enjoying the applause, while above the icon that is Alessandro on the production posters, crashes through the picture frame. The boy returns to the stage, dressed as a technician in time to push the paint frame off into the wings, like a wounded shopping trolley to reveal twenty Spanish dancers led by Pedro standing in frozen formation.

The music changes to a Spanish Bolero and the dancers, all in perfect synchronicity, bang their instruments and fix their eye lines at the front of the stage. The boy leaves the stage and stores the paint frame by the quick-change room where he sits in the wings to get his breath. Claire nods a silent greeting and joins him to watch the dancers together. She reaches across to his legs and he freezes as she places her hand on his inner thigh. The boy looks not to her but at Anita who is watching them from the other side of the stage. When the dancers reach a crescendo, Alessandro appears from one side of the stage to the other, to reveal that he is half man and half woman. He tangos with himself from stage left to right as the dancers complete the complicated routine. Across to the other-side of the stage he, with Anita's help, changes his presented mask. The boy wants her to want him again, yet she is on a pathway further from the boy's love that cannot return. At the end of his act, Alessandro pulls a string and his suit turns inside out and as if by magic the black tails, now white, take centre stage alongside the bull headed boy who kicks the last tambourine high into the air, back flips and catches it on the last beat of the music.

From the bandstand, a new tune plays, mesmerised the Waiters down tools and start singing. They walk to the front of the stage and turn to first face the dancers and then the audience. Their moves are amateurish and clumsy and most are showing off, led by Charles, who with no real ability, other than to camp up everything, earns his minute of fame. The forestage lifts and just at the point of ecstasy it then descends, as it does every night, returning the waiters to their rightful place, ready to serve the dessert course. The song is finished with a jive interlude and the waiters watch, sorbets in hand, as the professionals twist in absolute perfection. The audience applaud and Alessandro does not disappoint them. He clicks his fingers and the curtain rises, revealing a set describing Frankenstein's laboratory. A cloak is thrown to Alessandro who dresses and puts on a top hat from on top of a coffin. He calls out and the band changes the music to a theme of horror. Francine runs out, dressed in a white night shirt and awkwardly impersonates a virgin. Alessandro grabs her hand and pulls her to him ready to deflower her virtue for the audience's pleasure. Hugo appears from behind the coffin, dressed in a lab coat and pulling faces that detract from the scene. Alessandro picks out a sword from a rack on the wall. Hugo takes a watermelon from the coffin and throws it into the air for Alessandro to expertly slice it in half with the flashing blade. The audience gasp with Francine as he turns the blade to her. She screams a second time and he plunges the same sword into her body. The blade, switched with a trick, penetrates through to her back and then she revolves in a slow dance with Alessandro as he cuts backwards and forwards through her flesh. Alessandro removes the steel and she falls into Hugo's arms, laying her prostrate body wedged into the coffin. Alessandro places her inside with her head outside the box. Her feet are left protruding at the other end. Hugo produces a spinning circular saw that splinters the box in half, accompanied by the screams of both Francine and squeamish members of the audience. The box is then separated for Hugo to walk through and lick the imaginary wounds. When the box is reunited, Alessandro sprinkles his magic glitter over the box. With the magic completed, Francine bursts out from her prison, returned to her earlier virginal state. She tries to run and Hugo catches her hand and throws her to Alessandro who ties Francine to a rack. He pulls a curtain around her and she is gone from the audiences' sight but, still screaming. The illusion ends with an ironic switch, Francine walks forward in a new costume with her captor tied to the rack. Hugo rushes over to reveal Alessandro, tied up, with a line of blood trickling down his mouth. The front curtain drops and Alessandro is removed from his capture. The blood, although an effective addition to the illusion, is not a fake but as real as the pain that goes with it.

    The music vamps an upbeat change and the actors separate from the stage to their next scene. Francine calls for Anita, who with the available theatre technicians, usher Alessandro to his dressing room. Anita ignores all others and tends to her charge, while they resume positions for the next scene. In the dressing room she removes his clothing and calls for a doctor on the house telephone. Despite losing Alessandro, the show has to continue and Hugo takes the centre stage to play his piano, while the crew dismantle the flats of the laboratory scene and remove the props. A forty-foot piano is lowered onto the stage behind him, while in front of the cloth Hugo presents his Jerry Lee Lewis tribute. This is always popular and Jo, the deputy stage manager, looks across from her cue box to watch him with pride. The piano scene finishes in an explosion giving a visual cue to the technical crew to lift the curtain. In the frame of the stage is a grand piano. An intricate piece of music plays from the band and a dancer pretends to depress the massive piano keys. Alessandro usually plays the piano, but he has still not returned from his dressing room. Joel has stepped in to play the scene, keeping the audience unaware of the problems backstage. Dancers trip lightly over the piano lid, tap dancing and back flipping. On cue the lid lifts to reveal the girls who jump up from inside and complete an intricate tap step that mirrors the honky-tonk music of the band. They dance to a tune especially written for the show, a parody of the 'Black Bottom' from the 1920's. The whole company dance the 'Charleston', in a period sequence full of lively syncopation. The audience by this time are out of their seats and before their coffee arrives they are dancing with the waiters and each other. The models walk down through the dancers dressed in the expensive and revealing costumes of opulent promised sex. Alessandro is not the only one to miss the finale.

During the Hugo piano sequence, first aid and an ambulance have been called. Ellen is not missed in the walk down and Denny steps deftly into her shoes for the rest of the run. Alessandro is hidden in his dressing room; Anita attends to him, placing warm towels over his shivering body as the stage manager summons the theatre doctor. By the following day he is given permission to return to repeat his performance, the pills have been discarded and the seizures have ceased. The last number completes the evening performance and the company take a bow and encore the last tune. The curtain falls as the band finish their last bars of music on from the scores, while the audience prepare for the cabaret with their coffee.

It is the end of the show for this night. The audience drink liqueurs before leaving. Some will want more and stay for the cabaret. The backstage is cleared until the next morning, leaving a skeleton staff to manage the band for the evening. Nobody asks about Ellen, but her clothes sit waiting for collection at the stage door. By 2 am, even the cabaret has left and it is quiet at the theatre. Everyone has gone, until tomorrow.

EPILOGUE

2008

I am the show. I am the sum of all the energies that make up the product that is called the production. I watch and also perform. I have the perspectives of every person that takes part in the show. I have their collective memories to keep me alive beyond the end of the run. If you did want to know, the magician still appears regularly in the Parisian nightclubs. He is a star name, an international celebrity that is often seen on the television, taking the space where Jean Paul Reme would have sat. Alessandro is now 49 years old and a confirmed bachelor. He wears his make up, to hide his lined face and in public still appears as the flamboyant character, rather than the mouse he really is. To keep his flying illusion safe, he keeps a strict regime and has never lost the figure that he had twenty-four. The few dark years of depression have gone, but so has the youthful enthusiasm for the magic. Alessandro's time in England was just a part of his life, a chapter that has made his fortune. When he visits Brazil, there are young nephews who ask him to teach them the illusions. They will be the new audience, who are tricked by his manipulation of coins and animals. The family are less inclined to protect their children from this man, and he has found peace in the community who once doubted him.

Anita, finished her contract in London and moved back to South Africa, where she works for a local TV network, making the costumes for a multi-racial soap opera. She does not keep in contact with the people of London, as they are thousands of miles from her mind.

The prop boy is now a man and his children ask him to tell them stories about his life as a magician's assistant. The love he had for the dresser is still inside him, locked and never opened. His daughter in France has grown to be beautiful, but he does not know of her. She walks the fashion stages of Paris. If she is asked about her family, she says that her mother walked from Angola to Morocco and then took a boat to France. That her mother appeared in the fashion shows in the early 1980's and then went to London to appear in a musical, before returning to Paris to have a baby.

Ronnie has always been working in the West End and his recent work is musical adaptation of the hanging of Daniel Bentley. He has high hopes for funding from the Leighton group and has arranged a showcase at the Bridewell Theatre with Mandy pencilled in for one of the roles.

Mandy still tours with 'Blood Brothers' and is seeking advice from a London Plastic surgeon.

Michael Leighton watches the West End from his office at the Regent Theatre, surrounded by pictures of his past theatrical successes. He still attends to the family business and is preparing to mount another popcorn musical. He has never married and now has a lover, who resembles a singer he once loved.

Hugo and Jo moved to Paris, between raising a family, they have penned some of France's favourite pop tunes, one which represented France at Eurovision 1998. Success and love are their deserved luxury.

Francine and Julian married in 1985, in a small ceremony in Paris. Their union lasted two months and Julian used his part of her wealth to establish his own theatrical ventures, while Francine now lives in Montpellier and keeps a colony of cats as her companions.

Dieta moved down to Brighton to live near the fresh sea air. He sometimes talks about a partner, an actor who is now long since dead. Dieta sells antiques from a market stall in the Lanes and specialises in theatre programmes from the great musicals.

Tracie lives in Ipswich and attends a clinic most weekdays. She left London in 1993, when she received the diagnosis, but has been treated successfully and can still be seen playing gigs at 'The Flag' public house, every first Thursday in the month.

Zute has never made his mark, has changed his name to 'Otis' and still plays the circuit in the hope, even in his fifties, of finally making it in the music industry.

Joel achieved an Open University degree and now works as a Social Worker in Mid Glamorgan. He wants to foster and probably will do a great job, if the authorities deem him suitable.

Dominic has had a second comedy series commissioned on BBC 2, which he co-wrote and in which he stars. He often appears on talk shows and his name is often mentioned whenever cutting edge comedy is discussed.

The Headwaiter Charles joined the cabin crew of Ryan Air and fulfilled every stereotype, before succumbing to HIV in 2006.

Ellen still lives in the 25th anniversary year of the production. James returned to live with her and Jack in their old house. Ellen slowly declines each day, but attends the yearly re-unions of the show while she can.

ANECDOTAL EVIDENCES

SHORT STORIES FROM THE PROPS BOY'S NOTEBOOK

Index

Jayanti's Night Out	1
Sixty Meters	2
life's movie	3
James Bond	4
Mocha and the Birth of Insects	5
Dance School	6
Tokyo Night	7
Roof of the World	8
Hartman	9
Conflict zone	10
Payment of Sorts	11
Oxymoron	12
Xmas Eve Guernsey	13
Birth and death	14
Waking to the Morning After	15
The Park 1976	16
A Bridge to Fear	17
Case History of 'J'	18
Magic in the home	19
Letter to Martha	20
Tree of love	21

Jayanti's Night out

Jayanti sat by her dressing table mirror and waited for her hair tongs to heat up. It was the night after her most successful of days at work. She had sold a fourth house in as many days. The highlighted spreadsheets, showing completed sales and the time they take to finalize. As the end of year sales were added up, Jayanti now had the chance for promotion and her chance in branch Management.

The hair tong's, were a by-product of Jayanti's attempts to conform to another society. The natural bounce to her silken black locks did not formulate into the slick moulded shape required by the latest styles and the electric help has helped her cheat each morning to the visual conformity in the branch. While certain colleagues were aiming the romantic sights at the current Branch Manager, Jayanti had already bagged the catch. Alistair was seemingly captivated by her culture. Jayanti was flattered and intrigued to follow her boss away from the professional path. She now had more status and it was a corruption that gave her pleasure intellectually as well as carnally.

If this relationship was known in her office it would have caused a minor diplomatic incident, Jayanti liked having the secret. By carefully avoiding the work squabbles, she had used her determination to close many a deal, Jayanti was destined for greater things. She still felt different to the others a Smith Patterson Estate Agents. When the Muslim outrages were discussed openly Magda placed Jayanti, a Hindu, into the same religious category, snidely suggesting that she had something of an affinity to that cause. Since Jayanti's prophet was as far removed from Mohamed, this normal Xenophobia did not shake

Jayanti's resolve to harmony. Inwardly she has never forgotten the comments, or the true intended sentiment. The faith, she worked into her life had discrepancies to her lifestyle, but she still believed that Krishna would save her immortal soul in the end. Jayanti lived in a ramshackle Terrace owned by her family and the business they run. Inadequate for the extended family that lived within its walls, she has never complained about the lack of privacy and independence. While showing young white couples around penthouses, she has never wished to leave these roots, until such time as she can provide for her whole family.

In the house she has a shared living space with Pretty her elder sister. They have spent their whole lives together, secretly and knowingly growing. Pretty is only ten months her senior and attends the local university studying the Social sciences that will provide another female professional in the second generation. They expect then that she will be married soon followed by Jayanti to men of their parents choosing.

There are two brothers Jiyma and Sandip, who are working in the family shop, content to build empires of an outward display. They live the same second-generation life and have no fear of being caught for they will have a chance to repent when they finally settle down. The hair tong is a shared purchase with Pretty and Jayanti, a joint secret, as are the cosmetics that they keep hidden from the older family members. The girls combine all their paints and gadgets, the same way they hide their behaviours that would compromise father's approval.

Tonight Jayanti has arranged with her father that she and Pretty will be visiting a colleague from her sister's University to exchange course materials. The girls will leave the house at a reasonable hour and walk to a closed space where they will reveal their true selves from a secreted bag of lip-glosses. They will then take a bus to the other side of the town and separate. Pretty intends to see her boyfriend at the University debating society and Jayanti has made arrangements to visit the wine bar to meet with Alistair, her regional manager. Alistair has no idea of the trouble Jayanti has taken to disguise the liaison, nor has she comprehended the deception this to his wife.

Alistair's own deception started at work when he called, in full view of Magda and Jane, the wine bar and made a booking for two. He then called his wife and told her blatantly that he was showing a client around a loft conversion, which could only be done at this hour, due to the client's busy schedule. The wife ended her conversation without complaint and Alistair could hear the cork leave another sweet white wine ready to be poured into her glass. Alistair leaves Magda and Jane to lock up the branch, he winks at them as he leaves and they swoon thinking that it, if only they had the opportunity, it could be their night. They regret their own companions, whose idea of tête-à-tête is switching off the television before penetration.

After work at Jayanti's terrace house the girls are mid preparation, there is a knock at the door.

'Father!'

Pretty hopped over the bed, deftly shutting the bag of cosmetics before she betrays them both. Jayanti places the heated tongs under the bed to hide discovery.

'Girls, Girls! Your mother and I shall send a cab to collect you at the gates of the University, I shall send Sandip to meet you both at 9:30pm, be in the reception area on time he has a busy night, with many bookings'.

The girls in chorus chant the expected answer that every father wishes to hear.

'What is that smell?'

'It is an incense stick father' says pretty rescuing the heated tongs from the matted and burned nylon carpet.

Reassured he leaves them, safe in the knowledge his girls will not disrespect their family.

Jayanti and Pretty, fully presentable, leave the house and in the shade of a bus shelter and add the extra colours to their faces. As they walk down the street Jayanti shows her sister the Estate Agent signs of the houses that she has sold. Proud of these sales, it will bring her rewards that her family have not known in this generation. But inwardly, she is not happy to sell other people's homes for the company's profit. Alistair parks his Audi A8 outside the 'Cheam Toad Wine Bar'. He smokes a cigarette and leaves the engine running. Jayanti and Pretty separate, one to the University and the other to her lover. Then the world stops. Just for a second, a saving second for Jayanti and Alistair to think of their futures. Alistair's phone rings and it is his wife. He switches off the engine and begins to cry, crying for the mess that becoming his life. At that same moment, Jayanti stops walking to the wine bar as she pictures an empty future with the man who she does not love. Turning back she calls to her sister who welcomes the company. No harm done.

Sixty Meters

Air brushes my cheek, cold clammy and distant air that has fed me inside this closed space. When enclosed, our minds can either focus on security or react against the restraint. Choice is not a word I would use to describe this present moment. This is what is called a predicament, and if it is a predicament, it is mine. For I chose to climb into this crevice, I chose to slip into the space between two dampened rocks and I presumably have chosen to stop breathing when the air, the little air around me finally goes. I am buried, and not in the conventional way. I did not dig down the customary six feet, this is not a manmade environment, a space of solid ground in which a box of bones would be slid ceremoniously, accompanied by the moans and quaffs of friends and family. This space existed, has existed for years before I was even life. When I turn my head, the only movement that remains to me are the lines of sedimentary silt describing the centuries and seasons.

    I climbed into the space, dressed for every known eventuality, hat, waterproof coat and a flash-light, the light, which now pulses a dull threat as it nears the end of its useful life. Enthusiastically I went into the earth, through compressed minerals and dust, followed only by the cold water and cooling air that followed me to the subterranean. Darker and deeper I am now through areas of natural and yet unnatural protection, above the world left breathing, absent of shelter.

    Our forbears lived like this, existing in caves that were hidden in a sanctuary of safe darkness with pools of water adding a source of life under the ground, the crudest of plumbing. Hair and animal skins help keep the early humans warm while fires, fed by the collected wood, feed the occupants with warmth and heat meat to taste. These caves have long since been left by man and beast and only recently, have the intrepid, dressed as explorers, fallen beneath ground level to become entombed for pleasure. There is a contact to my old world above. A line, sixty metres of nylon let out as I descended away from view, a colourful chain that has been stretched snagged and severed by something in the gap between the outside and my resting place. As there is no light, my world is only that which I can touch. It becomes closer. If I want to see my return, I can only feel the still cool supply of air seeping down to me. If I was able to slither like smoke, I could follow the trail to safety, but nothing now moves and I am as solid as the ground that holds me. I wish to touch the rope and this makes me know there is someone at the other end. I believe that above there should have been a warning. One never descends alone in to un-cloistered hell without a friend on the outside. They will be watching out for me and assessing my future. If they cannot help me, then they will call up the ladder to another level of rescue. This will be at the end of that sixty-metre rope and I will know nothing of it. All will wait above, a restraint of their own holding them to the phone or peering into the gloom, saying their prayers, while remaining safe themselves. When I am found there will be rejoicing, a hero's return and a retelling of the story with embellishments of the drama to pass on to yet to be conceived generations. You see I am being fed by positive thoughts now. It is the air that gives me hope. Then the water starts to trickle. Outside it must be raining, raining hard, for down it comes to find a path to a lower table, my table and cuts off the little air that was being piped to me. Oxygen is replaced by two thirds of hydrogen and as I have yet to learn how to breathe water, so I begin to choke.

    They will dig me out to then re bury me at a time more fitting, when all who know me can attend at a place more fitting. Sleep tight.

Losing the plot in life's great movie:

When we are young, we believe that the older person is wise and the years that have imbued the person with experience. My Grandfather qualified in his capacity for surviving the passing years. In the Eighty-Eight Circular years, he marked each with another line to his for head, another crease to his chin and another blotch to his once handsome features, if I believe the faded photographs.

My Grandfather did not continue developing beyond his retirement. As a child I saw the strong man, who during the week worked in his office in London and at the weekend would roll up his sleeves and mend his beloved Ford Consul. When he finished the work he would stand, stripped naked to the waist and wash in the sink with steaming water and blocks of carbolic, frothed into a frayed flannel. He was proud of his muscular body. Sixty years ahead of his youngest relative, he could not imagine that he would shrink to nothing in the matter of a decade.

Grandfather would show us his strength by picking up boxes in one hand and reach at shelves above the lines of clouds. He would always tell us that he came from a long-lived family and this knowledge allowed him to smoke a pipe in the confidence that he would not succumb, as other men of his age.

Grandmother was old as long as I could remember her. She creaked at every move and told horror stories to anyone who would listen about the degeneration of her body. This began the day she gave birth to the first of her three children, two of whom are still surviving and on the brink of middle age. She sat, rather than stood, spoke with a fever rather than soft breath and then cried whenever she did not get a modicum of sympathy from others. She was always on the point of dying and spoke often of the prospect and how she intended being dispatched and with which company she felt confident to bury her with enough gravitas as she felt she deserved. At Sixty-five, the office gave my Grandfather a watch and his very reason to wake at six am each morning was taken from him. He was no longer had a reason to fix his Consul for now never needed it to get him to work. He became a depositary for his Grandchildren and his role became that of a childminder, an experience he found to be an irritant. My Grandmother began to forget her ills and she took strength from his inadequacies. She became the queen in the home holding the balance of power, once held by the man in her life as his health dwindled.

'Tell us about the journey you made from London to Scotland with the war plans?'

Questions from the grand children confused him and each time he was asked, he remembered less. Grandmother would cover the gaps and we noticed little until we were older. Grandfather would nod in agreement as Grandmother finished the story with a moral twist that bore no relation to the original events. Grandfather became less of a giant and as the seasons passed, we grew and he shrank. He no longer wanted us to be in the kitchen while he stood undressed in front of the porcelain washbasin. The gas water heater began failing, its flame giving an intermittent heat that scalded his receding skin. The car began to rot from beneath and in time the Consul was taken for scrap. He no longer drank tea from a Pint mug and his teeth fell out and became linked in a plastic band that Grandmother cleaned each night in a glass.

He did not notice, but we did. We saw that all memories had left the man. We saw that his depleted frame took longer to reach and he now asked for us to reach for him. Grandmother now accompanied him on every outing, she finding energy in his dependence. As he needed and shrunk, she straightened. Every personal assistance, he was given he gave up another virtue. To see vibrancy decay and the man I loved and wanted to become, swim across unknowing water made me question, what was the point of his experiences and his long life? Grandmother was always telling us sayings, 'A drowning person sees life pass before their eyes,' and I was reassured that all that he had felt in his eight-eight years would return back to him in those last few moments.

He developed pneumonia and drowned in his own body fluids. He had a smile on the craggy sunken face and I believe to this day that the images that passed through his eyes must have been good ones. As I age. I will not try and live in my past. I shall wait, as did my Grandfather, until my end, when I shall live my whole life in the Technicolor movie that will be me.

James Bond

'James Bond, with two double Bourbon's inside him, sat in the final departure Lounge of Miami airport and thought about life and death.'

<u>Gold finger by Ian Fleming.</u>

While waiting in the departure lounge, Jane became immersed in the pages of the book she was reading. The one she held in her thin fingers was from her usual, if yet unconventional reading list. She read the opening sequence of 'Gold-finger' and thought back to the film version musing on which of the characters she was about to impersonate, it depends on her mood, her location and the chapter. So if she had been at home stroking her cat, she could picture herself as a balding megalomaniac with a scar across one eye, she did not like the character but could empathise with the man's love of felines. Sometimes when stepping from her shower she would imagine herself as Ursula Andres walking from the seas her 'Pussy Galore' ready to attract the debonair James. She does not have the body of Ursula Andres for Jane is round as a beach ball and her hair is mousy and thinning. She is not a James Bond but would like to be. It is just Jane and a plain Jane at that, sitting at the departure lounge at Gatwick awaiting the shuttle service back to Edinburgh.

The terminal buildings could be Miami; they all look the same air conditioned and clinical. Stepping again into the pages and living her fantasy, she could be one of the Russian agents sent to help James on a mission, in disguise as a minor Civil servant in the East Strydshire planning office. Jane need not dream intrigues, for even this Jane has secrets and a mission to complete. She reads another sentence of Bond's assignment. Jane, like her hero, is returning to a crisis, there will be dangers and she will have to take a side that she believes is for the good. Her mission is not like James Bond's and her actions are not for queen or country. The world order does not hang in the balance, nor will a despot dictator play evil games with the world's future, held in the balance of his warped mind. Her battle involves the politics around local park bench placements, appeals for pelican crossings, planning applications and local eyesores that need demolishing to improve the views for the residents. There are no nuclear proliferation struggles in her story, no evil intentions at destabilization of political governments. Her world is not the same as is in the Novel she reads.

She is drawn to this literary covert world as she feeds from it. She has fantasies that she is living in a similar territory. On the outside she is an innocent directive for town planning but in reality is a spy uncovering the seedy side of local government, which she can topple and in doing, topple councils! How would James Bond operate in the East Strydshire Highland Council Planning Office? If Gold finger were a developer, planning a new secret underground headquarters and approached James Bond, local Planning Officer, (Licence to Build.) for planning permission. How would he justify asking for a huge cavernous dome that explodes at the end of chapter 14, what would be the scenario? There would be professional challenges. It would have been inconceivable in current building laws, for that sort of property to get planning consent in real life. Just thinking of the environmental nuisance that it would cause during the construction, let alone the imbalance it could cause to local providers of facilities. Think of the water supply needed just to maintain the sewer system required for a thousand hired henchmen. If it did get the permission due to some underhand dealings by the master criminal, would James Bond be as likely to lead a small army of allied crack commandos to blow it up, knowing how much preparation and tendering the build would take to construct. Jane sighed as she does when her fantasy and reality worlds collide. James Bond would not live in her world, so she must not live in his. In the world of the East Strydshire Planning department, people do not make such demands. There are no real colourful characters in Town Planning, only quietly corrupt individuals in amongst the majority of law-abiding civil servants.

Jane has a secret. She too has a mission and while the world thinks she is travelling incognito as Jane Maund, Planning Officer of East Strydshire County Council, in reality she is a plant sent by another organisation to unearth a corruption that her people will use to topple the present controlling regime at the next May election.

Jane also has a Nemesis, an evil other who is ready to break her without care or compassion in the name of a belief that his greed is good. This Man was at the conference with her. He is now sitting opposite her in the airport lounge, not reading but picking his teeth and smugly reliving his finest hour as representative of his party in government. Even if his present domain is local government planning, he is behaving a little like Gold-finger. Kelvin Proctor, Chief Local Planning Director (Conservative) chuckles insanely to himself while he combs his Spartan hair around a podgy bloated face. Why is Kelvin her nemesis? Does he have links to the fiendish underworld? Are the minions that he controls armed to the teeth and willing to die in his service, while wearing ridiculous ill fitting all in one cat suits? I think not.

Kelvin Proctor is only the controller of the small party led council planning department, yet he has ultimate power and this power has begun to corrupt him. Kelvin does not have a hidden HQ, nor does he have a shark pool. His office does sport a fish tank, but the Guppies within are harmless. He does have a hidden filing cabinet, which holds his illegal transactions however he is unlikely to use genocide as a means to protect his enterprises. Jane is Kelvin's assistant and she types his correspondence, eats, drinks and on one occasion has slept with him. She believes that by turning the tables on Kelvin it is for the good of the party, but not his party and her mission is to provide the political opposition meat to their campaign at the by-election. While Kelvin believes she is loyal to his future aspirations and the party allegiance, in reality she has been disclosing his shady deals ready for the final attack and destruction of the sordid little world the Planning Office has become. Kelvin will soon be disgraced and she will cross back to her true party and be welcomed by her controller, who will congratulate her for her skilful handling of the mission. East Strydshire's Planning Office will be, once again in the safe hands. No one suspects Jane. She is the perfect spy. Recruited at her university, they recognised that she would be a perfect turncoat. Jane hides her true colours under her poncho, and she hates the colour blue with a passion. Jane had friends infiltrated high political Planning offices and they helped her procure the post to help the opposition. Jane also harbours the Directorate, Kelvin Proctor, a grudge. For her time at the local Grammar school, Jane had been marred by a school bully and it is this same Kelvin Proctor, who now employs her who was that bully. It is he who is now already making headway in political circles and destined for corruption at a higher level. Jane committed herself to working covertly for the opposition council, both for the love of revenge and the cause of righteousness. The opposition planned for her to work as a sleeper, amass the much-needed information and then disclose it at the appropriate moment, for to cause the best negative effect to the party in power. Kelvin needs an assistant as he lost in his office without help and Jane was installed after an interview, in which she fawned and proclaimed that she had always had a crush on the dashing boy in her school. Kelvin was as easily corrupted by a compliment and her willingness to say yes to his ambitions. Jane followed Kelvin, obtaining evidence and placing such mistakes in the files that would build up a suitable case to undermine his professional foundations. Tonight it will all happen. Tonight they are returning from the party conference, taking the shuttle flight to home after a weekend of political flag waving. Kelvin has basked in the weekend of Schmoozing, sea and hotel sex and is now ready to prepare for government again at the start of the May election trail. Kelvin feels good, buoyed up by the release from his loins with the woman sitting before him reading her book. Kelvin hardly remembers her from his school days, he bullied so many, and it was hard to recall individuals. Jane's sexual compliance over the weekend was a suitable finish to the networking. After he had been plied with the free party drink he found himself at the end of a night with need of a mate to round off the event. The girl was, he thought an easy conquest and would have been grateful of the experience. This smugness will make Jane's final deathblow all that sweeter.

They will return to find the deed done. Kelvin, while riding high on the wave from meeting his political idols, will fall spectacularly. He had thoughts of one day being a leader and enjoying the perks to that occasion. But Jane is ready to pull the plug on Kelvin's ambitions? She did spend the night under him. Pinned to the sheets by his sweating drunk odour and then spent an hour in her own shower scratching his scent from her skin. She kept telling herself that she was serving the cause and this detachment helped her endure the swift completion of Kelvin's limited recreation.

'I think it was a most successful weekend, don't you?' Kelvin stops Jane's train of thought, his confidence grows as his wandering hand touches her knee. 'We should have a drink before the flight loosen us both up, busy day ahead tomorrow.'

Jane knew that he did have a heavy schedule, meetings that would he thinks be with other party faithful, yet if all goes to plan it will involve a police raid on the inner office and publicity of his shame.

'How 'bout that drink?' His persistence stems from his thoughts of a potential drunken copulation in the clouds between Gatwick and Edinburgh coupled with the deals he will engineer when he retains his seat in local government.

'A Martini would be nice', says Jane turning a page but not directly making him eye contact, lest he should suspect her motives.

The end is always the same for James Bond. He sets an elaborate trap for the villain, while being a prisoner within the evil organisation. In the midst of the destructive chaos, James not only escapes without a hair out of place, but allows a thousand allied commandos to trample through the evil lair to destroy the doomsday device and safe guard the world peace. James's reward is to escapes on a life raft with a beautiful maiden. In the book, 007 and his mistress indulge in unprotected, yet harmless sexual intercourse before being winched back to civilisation, government congratulation and the roulette table. Jane does not have a lover awaiting her successful completion of her mission. She might impress some of the party faithful, but they will not make this spy their own. She will probably not have a job after the balloon goes up, and her time in East Strydshire's Planning office will be just a distant memory of her covert past. In hours her true identity will be revealed and she, the spy in the camp, will have done what she was commissioned to do. That is reward enough. The drink arrives and she stirs rather than shakes the Martini, knowing that she is breaking a convention and accepting a gift from the man she will soon expose.

MOCHA and the Birth of Insects

Your pupa hatched in the south midlands town of Cheltenham and as with many of your days it was spent flying around looking for food and laying your own eggs, where you interact with humans. Today we are watching thirsty human tourists looking at the Regent scenery. On this hot summers afternoon you follow people towards a café to sup a sugary meal. You look around with your many eyes, and seeing a coffee house you change direction and fly in. Located down the upmarket district of the town and tucked behind the ornate gothic and Georgian square we insects join the guzzling few. There is warmth drawing us in, the smell of food and the company of other insects, calls to our clan. On the wall are the paintings and photographs, art with intentions to commercial gain all priced and likely to remain in the possession of the artist. The counter, situated on the left-hand side contains cakes and sweets. Behind the Counter are three people, two girls are working, making, preparing and serving. Two of them smile and attend to the queue of customers. There is a tall man wearing a similar halter apron, he does not engage with anyone. He does not even look up from his thoughts.

Fly at ceiling level through the coffee house you arrive in the second room. People here seem to be reading the Broadsheet papers, the Guardian or the Times perhaps, for you seldom get a tabloid reader in these premises.

Another fly comes closer to one of the cups by one of the tables and is dispatched by the fist of customer, who finds invertebrates an intrusion to his coffee enjoyment. The animal caught in the down draft is maimed and then quickly dispatched by a paper, 'Blessings to the fallen comrade!

Be careful, for this is an inhospitable environment and in the loss a fellow soldier is a reminder to us to be vigilant. The owner of the coffee shop, the man in the apron preoccupied in his thoughts, he is thinking about his lover who has left him to set up home with someone else and he despises this rival. The girls at the counter ignore his mood, not yet knowing of the domestic situation of their boss. They take the orders and are serving with efficiency that is not modelled by their employer. A customer comes into the café. Not the type of customer that would naturally fit into this setting. He orders himself the simplest beverage, a black weak tea. He has a usual seat in the corner within view of the counter, which gives him ample opportunity to stare at one of the young girls serving.

He feels incongruous in this cafe, yet he is thirsty and like the rest of us, he likes to sit in amongst the other classes to find refreshment. We hang upside down on the ceiling and watch him watching her. Jack, the café owner takes off his apron and without talking to his colleague's walks out to the front to smoke.

At the nearside table, this man sits drinking his tea. He cannot look away from one of the girls and the point of his tongue extends expectantly while he watches one of them, in selection. The man with the tea pretends to read while he watches the counter. He glances at her, snatching a picture of his favourite girl working behind the counter, watching her serving the customers and furtively gazing at her top. We watch him and in multi vision see his intentions before he makes a move.

Each time she froths a beverage; he can just spy her leaning forwards and savour, with his eyes the well-exposed breasts. The girl knows she is being watched and is used to being the man's eye candy. Natasha is her name, at twenty-four she has a life of experience, a university degree that has yet to be tested and a body she is proud to flaunt. She does enjoy the look that some males give her and yet complains that it is the only reason she as been employed. Natasha cannot reconcile with the idea of wearing more modest clothes and sees it as her right to dress, as she wants. Now and again, there is the occasional customer that can melt her resistance. But not that man watching her, he is not that customer. Natasha is getting on well with the boss but is not thinking of developing their relationship beyond the counter. Her mind returns to her uncertain post-graduate future and cursing the economy, for reducing her to being employed as a coffee girl. Natasha tries to forget the man in the suit and says to Bonny, her colleague in the café, 'I like your nail varnish.'

'Thanks' says Bonny 'it's a new blue but I wasn't sure I liked it or not.'

Natasha looks across at the man in the suit who is now peering over the paper. 'You know . . . like I don't like that customer, yea. I always think he is looking at my tits.'

Bonny stops admiring her fingers, 'Oh yeah, he probably is, so?'

Then another customer comes in and they switch focus to present the company's greeting and service. The man sipping his black tea is 32 years old. He has a job as a research assistant in the local council and is now and again employed by the university as part time a fiction writer, unpublished. His name is Paul Davies. His father is Welsh and his mother is from the Breton regions of France. He speaks with a slightly middle class South Wales accent and his pronunciation of French is definitely authentically Gallic due to his mother's roots. He reads mystery and occult novels and his writing impersonates this genre. Paul is fond of a certain kind of Thrash rock, he keeps this to himself and comes into the cafe on a regular basis, to gain inspiration and study the girls. If you stay here long enough, you will see him on subsequent days, in the same seat, looking at the same view and tormented within for he is fixated on Natasha, without knowing her name. He fantasizes that she is a graduate and looking for a mate. He thinks that she must be between 25 and 30; a student perhaps in fine arts, English or sociology. He has no real knowledge of Natasha, other than that he has invented about her. He thinks she might be an occasional feminist, keen to put down men, yet encouraging them with her dressing to exploit their sexual needs. There is a cake crumb spilt at the corner of table four, swoop down and feed on the sugar pastry, watch your back and listen to his thoughts. We invertebrates do not need language to understand. Without language thoughts are pure and easily read. He is thinking that he wants her for his own, yet his wishes will not fit her desires. In the dark recesses of the male fantasy Paul is dreaming of ownership and not a relationship with the girl at the counter.

See that unattended pastry down there at table six. If we are quick we can feast for a few seconds and lay a few more eggs upon its crystal topping. The pastry is good. So good that we are joined by two other comrades and a wasp who has intentions of invading our space. Natasha comes across and scoops up the plate, shooing us away from the glazing of honey and sweeteners. I suggest we fly towards the window and catch some of the setting sunshine. The wasp careers up to the neon light mesmerized by the hypnotic sheen and as we turn to the Eastern end of the café we hear a 'zap' as another victim falls We flies are not liable to remain long inside a café that boasts a 'bugzap 2000'.

Look behind, Paul is talking to Natasha. He has his eyes focused on her top as he speaks. He cannot look her in the eye, partly out of his shyness and possibly because she is showing him her cleavage at such a close quarter.

She dismisses him with the pleasantry that becomes a hostess and he leaves the counter with a second tea this time he has a polystyrene cup with a lid and a selection of pastries. The transaction completed Paul has little reason to stay and his seat has been taken. Where shall he go? Are we to remain here also, now they have killed two insects, for it is a 'Danger-Zone.' What is our plan then, when does a fly normally have a plan? Paul has a paper carrier bag containing sweet candies that make for our transport and his meal to go. Let us land there and tag along. Follow this failed lover, for he might be our next chance of a meal. Two of us dart down to the bag and climb in safe. Paul leaves the café and walks across to a basement flat, less than 100 yards away. It is a cheap rental that he can just afford in the more affluent area. Paul lives in the dankness and has grown used to the limited luxury that his home provides. He deposits the food on the kitchenette and goes into the front room where his personal effects are spread across the floor. In one corner of the bed-sitter is his single unmade bed and the other side a television and selection of DVD's marked with a code that he has personally devised. Paul drinks the tea but has no hunger and out of habit puts the television on. We wait inside the bag until we feel he is not interested in us and tentatively crawl out to watch him. He gets into his bed, fully dressed and setting the alarm watching the screen until his eyes close and his breathing becomes heavy.

After an hour the alarm goes off and he gets up, collecting his coat the pockets that contain the remnants of a Twix bar that he started eating earlier makes to leave. We are inside the coat pocket having afforded another lift and another free meal.

Paul leaves the basement and climbing to the street level, can see across the square to where the café is just closing up. Natasha and Bonny are kissing each other on the cheek preparing to return to their respective private lives. Paul pulls up the collar and walks across to the main road where he waits. He has done this before and knows the routine for the girl has a fixed pattern to her life that he has captured many times. Inside the other pocket of the coat contains a small digital camera. He switches on the camera unseen, as he removes it from his pocket he points the lens at the body walking towards him.

'Hello' he wants to say to her.

'Come to my home,' he wants to say.

'Spend a night with me,' he needs to say.

Natasha passes him without recognizing the customer, her attention is taken to another place by the ipod vocals in her ears. She does not notice the camera he is holding. Paul walks behind her as she crosses the main road, heading towards her digs in the fashionable student quarter of the town. It is not uncomfortable in the pocket for us fly's as we eat and discuss fly business. Outside the pocket Paul's camera invades Natasha's life. He knows where she lives and has repeated this journey many times. The edit of the discs, a composite expression of those visits and his desire to finish, finish the film. Finish the job. She turns into an alley and goes to her front door in the semi darkness. Natasha inserts her key oblivious to the world around her. In her ears pulsates the trash of James Blunts vocals warming her dreams for unobtainable love. This is the point where he pounces. The pockets empty in the struggle, the camera falls to the ground and us fly's buzz from the warmth of his coat to the cold outside night. The coat becomes a means to smother the girl, to prevent her fighting back. Fly up to the ceiling of her home and we can see the struggle. The man's body, however limited in its strength compared to other men, is still full of the chemical of dominance. Natasha is fighting back. She cannot see her attacker. She can smell his sweat and feels his hands pushing her to the floor. Paul pins her to the floor in blackness. Her light taken by the coat across her head, it divorces her from knowing her attacker. Then before removing the coat from her head, he takes a roll of tape from his trouser pocket and starts to bind her into the coat, then hands and legs. She stops struggling and lies twisted on the floor of her home awaiting the revelation. Paul is out of breath and panting. He stops when she is secure. Lets her go and pulls close the curtains. In the darkness he covers his own face with a black wool mask, and becomes himself invisible. Then he takes the coat off her and blinds her vision with a thick duck tape and binding her mouth with a gag. Her skirt is lifted up and he modestly pulls it down for the sight of her thigh shocks him a little. She tries to stretch but is held tight by the tape that binds her. He leaves her struggling in the blackness and walks to the kitchen and runs the tap. She cannot call out as her mouth is held closed by the tape, but we the insects hear her thought cries and fly down to her side. Walk across her body we welcome in support of the person soon to join us. Natasha is conscious that she is tethered. She still has the sounds of James Blunt in her headphones and to her dying day believed that her attacker had the voice of her fantasy lover. When Paul returns to the room, he has washed his hands and places his video camera on a stand in front of the body, which he will use to record their lovemaking. As he reaches her side she spasms and the breath leaves her, only a lifeless shell remains on the ground. He bends to his knees and touches her face. Underneath the mask the eyes are open and the light dances in the whites but she has left. We insects have grown by one.

'So you have joined us Natasha.' The woman Natasha has now become six legged and changed her shape to the silvered winged and three bodied insect before us. Natasha is no more and the body remains are the property of the state and the boy who cradles her sacking shell.

We are all free as the insects around us. She has become one with us. She can return with us to the café and join the many creatures in the pastry cabinet. It is why there are millions more creatures than people. We are the people that have been. We grow in numbers with every one that joins us. Paul cannot violate the body. He cannot cross the line and his film is ruined. The spent cartridge of film is wasted. Paul had planned to edit this final scene to honour her and then she escaped. All he has left is the final piece to camera and his slow walk to turn himself in to the police. Natasha watches him through her many eyes and knows that he will live the torment. He will face the authorities and then serve a term that will end his wasted life. He has made her into an insect, perpetually destined to live outside other humans. She can only hope that until he too dies, to become one of us, he too will live the hell that is being human and what little conscience he has left, will eat him from the inside until he leaves his shell.

Paul puts down his pen and considers whether the story should end here. He is startled from his thoughts.

'What are you writing?'

Natasha's face looks to the seated Paul Davies and across the small wooden table she crosses into his personal space.

'What is it that you are writing?'

Paul drops his eyes. His mouth is dry, even after the tea; it is not the dryness of saliva but the dryness of ineptitude, which stops him communicating. Natasha looks back at her colleague at the counter, acknowledging the game they are playing with him. Natasha's nod tells her friend that she intends to take this boy home with her and the nod in return makes approval of the choice. This man, Natasha has watched writing in his little notebook for the past hour, is all reserve, lacking in any outward ability to communicate, he sits with the papers of his fantastical story unread on his lap. She wants to read his diary that he is always writing when he is in the café. Natasha has decided that today she will read him and his words. Paul is sweating, for he fears that she cannot read the words, for the words will be the end of him. His fantasy is just that, a fantasy and the words he has written have no reflection on his true wishes.

'I will be finishing work in half an hour. If I get you another drink, will you wait for me?'

Paul nods his head. He needs another drink before his body turns into a dehydrated mass of dust. This is unreal for him, the dream is unreal and it is only when the tea arrives and he looks up to see her wink at him does he start to believe. The clock on the wall ticks through the next half hour. Time is now running at a slower pace. The hands held back. He cannot write anything and considers running out of the café. 'I'm ready!'

Natasha leads the way to the door. Paul follows silently behind her and walks into the spider's web.

Dance School

Anna, Lucy and Pippa put their collective feet to the bar at Madame Sabina's instructions. Their supple limbs stretched, clothing ligaments and muscles opened to new places while affecting the grimaces of childish innocence. Anna's toes curled at the base as she forced another 'inth of pressure onto her elevated foot. Lucy, with a dislocation, achieved a similar result and Pippa produced tears.

"Bodies that were designed to flex do not work well when they are torn from their sockets", spoke the orthopaedic surgeon to Pippa's mother who looked disparaging at the photograph presented to him. "I have seen many of these forms of dislocation and have subsequently treated such atrocities with plaster and traction, these experiments of dance are nothing but obscene. Degas images they are not!"

The damage was duly recorded and in due course Madame Sabrina's dance school received a closure notice.

"Told you I could stop the lessons," said Pippa, triumphantly to the admiration of Lucy and Anna, who equally hated spending every Saturday dressed as Swans.

Tokyo Night

In the early hours, the city stops moving. I am not one of the sleeping people for, after arriving from the opposite quarter of this planet it was inconceivable that I might wish to just sleep. Excitement had given me a second wind and in reverence of the fact, the experience that I had travelled further than I have ever been, further than anyone in my small recent acquaintance, I hold sleep at bay and soak up the night. When I am asleep I am as others, unreceptive to that around me, but awake I am special and in a special place, on one of many Islands east of the china seas. My hosts are asleep, the novelty of their location means little to them as they wake each day to their home. Their curiosity of this exotic place has waned through the years and as a consequence they can sleep soundly. They are naked, entwined together in the intense humidity high up on the mezzanine floor above the kitchen. Hanging on a single platform, levitating in slumber, they have chosen to be here. He a visitor turned resident and she born in the city and his companion and muse.

For me the strangeness of my present is a replica of my hosts experience many years before. When I, incredulous to the things I have seen, explode in words, he laughs at me seeing his own past. My excitement still has energy to burn and I need to see more of this culture.

Czardas and the constant hum of the electric wires melting the hot air, call me to the street. My covers shed I leave the wooden house and taking my boots from the outside, head towards the alien streets towards the heart of the city. I inhale the dense, humid night oxygen starved of freshness, awaiting a brewing storm. The streets of this suburb called Meguro were where prefabricated housing grew from the ancient fields, now service areas for the banking and diplomatic community. Within twenty minutes of walking I am at the centre, a cross roads of neon and people, even at the hour they are swarming through the pavements escaping the 24hour culture, as am I. Only I am invisible. I walk at a different speed and cannot stop while the over-speed around me did not notice the one western face. Twenty minutes later and I find sanctuary in a park.

As dawn approaches, I cross from asphalt of the cultivated city to the natural grass and soil. In one corner of the early morning a collection of workers are meeting. Without words they join, bow and place their belongings by their feet. Some have attaché cases, some plastic bags depending of their professions or occupation. They welcome me as they would anyone. There is no register, no formal arrangement, just a space and a leader with a modern tape machine. The leader starts its voice, polluting the calm of the first light with a discordant call. In another continent, this call could be a chant from a mosque or tolling bell to welcome the early worshipers. Despite the formality of the Shinto collective creed, here in the park there is no apparent religion, just a group who exercise before work as part of an ancient tradition of well-being. Although an interloper, I am now connected by this ceremony and became, for the present, a citizen.

Roof of the World

Each step takes me closer, the minute hand forcing a step in time with my pacing. The terrain has been selected, harsh gravel that is slow to treed and noisy reverberating through my feet. The machine that surrounds me is encompassing, the smooth outside belying the textures that it can produce in keeping with the script that I have programmed for it. As the walls seal, a bright light comes on and in the closed space of the pod the limits of its metallic geography cease to be. Holographic images, dimensionally projected give me a horizon, which permeates into a reality. Jets of air feed my lungs with the cold thinning air. As I progress upwards to the produced incline, I begin to believe that this is now real and my expedition is as real as I once remembered it. I could be joined, if I so wish it with anyone to accompany me. It is possible to create, one memory and their image is replicated in moving silicon that is warmed to the temperature of body heat.

To my right is a valley. The ravine that falls three hundred metres away is laid out in a conifer carpet, while to my left is a wall of rock that I will not touch, but sense that it is holding me to the side of this mountain. Ahead of me is three hours of struggle; the gravel beneath my walking boots is also a figment of my programme. I crunch the ground in a delayed time, calculated by the computer sound in digital, almost too real to my dampened ears. Pressure in the capsule is real prescriptive to that of the sea level and the GPS positioning I remember. I try to forget that I am still inside the simulator pod, it's replication is equalled to the reality, as long as I do not reach out, touch the walls, I can be fooled to the belief that, I am there, here with you. Forward, stretching upwards to the summit I push onwards. The floor, its feel and direction incline to the steep trail ahead of me. We are above the green line and in the no man land of green and white the journey reaches a limit. In a point of exhaustion I stop, governed by the machine. Experience has an edge; my feet are close to the corners of the track. I stare downwards to the moving feet, the spinning distances come up to find me, support me. When I chose to travel to this place I feared the dangers, animals that could climb from the caves to bite me, bandits that would hang from the trees, then drop across my path to debase and steal from the naive traveller. There was a joy in the real journey of reaching the end and safety. The reward of the journey was the magnificence of the view. The machine gives me the place and again rewards me with a view. I am a little disappointed that it is not exactly I remember when I recorded the experience. Clouds fall across the roof of the world, below horizons are lower than my feet and I am flying but solid on hard ground. I check the watch on my wrist, set to the time this once happened. Changeable cold cuts through me and I breathe deeply. When I first walked this journey, this was new and I was new to it. Exploration had a potential. I cannot experience a cold death again, not in the pod. Suddenly the mist clears and the winds change direction, the world sinks below and the sun, the sun of my creation cuts through the haze of evaporating water droplets. I can never be hurt here and so I step from the edge and fall, punching the air in front of me, falling downwards in a safe freefall.

Each history is within my grasp and I can re-live it whenever I have the yen to cover old ground. My machine is the living embodiment of my memories and built for the decaying body that now travels within it.

Hartman

Hartman focussed the dipped needle towards his arm. The result will be seen, when the light turns on. He has sketched the outline and a mark now needs to be made, together with puncture and pain.

Hartman is used to pain. He has plied hurt and discomfort on others for many years. It is his calling card and his experience of deploying torture is admired by others in his profession and copied by those less able. It is part of his legend. Hartman continues to hold the needle close to his arm. The ink drips venom that should by now, be turning flesh into decoration. These are living layers of his skin covering his tensioned muscles. On the wing, his body is admired by the other men but never touched, unless he wishes it.

The needle closes towards his arm, yet still Hartman cannot make contact. Scratched on the wall is the design and his arm is the clean canvas, shaved earlier in the shower block. His right hand hovers, the spike holding back the message that should be his tattoo. The ink has been stolen, so has the needle. Hartman will have to return the evidence after it has been used, or pay for their loss by giving up his trustee status.

There is a sigh from someone in the next cell as they read their mail and gently weep, while to his right, his other neighbour sings a hymn that grates with both God and man. As the chorus begins, Hartman presses the sharp point into his skin, penetrating and dividing the flesh that is alive and pale. He yelps then grits his teeth as he pumps the black liquid into his arm, words appear depicting his love. Each letter is a repeated pain and it is the first time that he understands that there is pleasure in receiving hurt.

When Hartman has finished and dried the sweat, when the smell of his urine has evaporated in his nostrils and when he has wiped the blood from the tool, he smiles and admires the name written on his body forever. 'M.U.V.E R'.

Conflict zone

She walked out through the doorway, white light, its ultraviolet sheen burning her face and hands. Dressed in white and holding aloft two flags, the heat breeze causing them to intertwine, this lone pedestrian is now a legitimate target. There is a flash and a building topples in shards of masonry. These warring nations do not dare to touch her and she continues away from their path. Above, the skies are broken by fire that emanates from the arse end of rockets and jet engines. For those at the launch it is another day and a job to be done. She wanders without a direction or map hoping that she will be guided to the line that separates two factions, except that line is constantly changing, as are the attitudes of those funding this current crisis.

I watch her walk, for she is now captured on the screen and her last moves recorded. As a foreigner, her life has value and she has given all that she has to be active in someone else's occupied land. Her statement is purely for propaganda, for as others it is revenge. At home, her parents are interviewed on the screen that I watch, immediate time relayed and an immediate commentary from those who care and those who follow her steps from the comfort of their homes. She has now turned to a street and faces a man holding a tube on his shoulder. He waves to her to pass him and his view. She waves back and her flag flows in the sun. He waves again and screams at her in a language alien to her western ear. In her euphoria she is recognising that she is part of this history and loves the man who holds the trigger. Her love is for all men and she now believes it should be thus. According to her parents, she turned her love away from them and gave it to a wider world, which led to this journey. By watching the screen, the world shares her personal news and thinks of its own children. We relish our son's and daughter's safety and how close we keep them from harm. We are watching others play this video game, but it is real, as observers to history no need to become physically involved. Behind her another faction appears and she turns to see a vehicle with flawless plate and fluid tracks approaching her and the man intent on destroying. It takes aim. She cannot see any faces as they are held inside the protection of steel. She does not need that protection and believes that she has 'right' protecting her shell. She too is as flawless as the armour directed past her and as destructive as the weaponry directed in return at the opponent. She jumps and does not stop flying. Her flags lifting her wrapped in the combined emblems of each country, she is taken back to her true home.

    I turn off the screen and pray.

Payment of Sorts

The toilet roll was a form of currency. We never bought them complete and even a square of the rolled tissue had a value. Light bulbs, either purchased at the local Spa, or removed from another property in the estate, were traded for anything. If the owner of the property had electricity, light was a resource that required the investment of a bulb. They however were very rarely needed in the packs of six and so an intermediary was employed to divide the items into manageable amounts.

Light bulbs, of course only have a value when there is a supply of electricity. In the top flat of the block the owner held the electric account, sharing his wealth to those who needed a supply for the fee he charged, with a length of industrial cable wire. The agent of this power was also the provider of everything else we needed. He divided the cannabis resin we slowly assimilated into our diet. In the evenings he took the block and with a heated knife separated weighted amounts for us at a price. When we returned to our cold dark flats, it was only because of him that we could put light into our homes so we could see, while we lit up the tobacco and resin, which gave us a limited escape.

I lived on the ground floor, in a space that adjoined the flooded remnants of one of the derelict properties. My home was water tight, but next door the Council workmen forced the water pipes to fracture, making the property uninhabitable. To prolong the inevitable damp I climbed in one night and rigged lengths of guttering to divert the constant supply of sewage and tap waters out of a one of the many broken windows. My own home remained dry while a stream of waste wound its way to the kerbside. I had moved into the estate and with my 100 metres of cabling, purchased a space in the shared fuse box from the flat above and begun to make it home. The views from the ground were of the riversides dull edge and only on the 3rd floor was a panorama of waterside industry. Views across the bend in the river facing the City in one direction, Greenwich in another and Wapping wharf opposite.

I made the area habitable with cast off furniture, a cooker and heater but no fridge my diet consisting mainly of fresh foods and tins purchased every other Tuesday when the cash giro was collected. I could not run many electric items. The distance, physics that I still cannot comprehend, lessened the power from my electricity supply, over the 100meter stretch from the flat above. When it entered my fuse box, it had enough power to create a dull glow to the bulbs that I supplemented by candles housed in empty wine bottles. My situation, like many of those around me was one of chosen poverty. Every person in the block is the fallen, hiding in the abandoned council estate, as escapees from our qualifications and ambitions, able but apathetic. My story is of little consequence, except to say that maybe someone needs to record those times. Tied to the flat above were many residents. One of other wires was Eddie; He was older than the rest of us in the estate. Elongated in stature and prematurely balding, which for a socialist, pained him more than it should. He was from Manchester and had an uncanny resemblance to the Lead singer in the Stranglers, an image he tried hard to cultivate. He became our political advisor, as the provider in the flat above us sustained our bodies, so Eddie fed our politicised minds. In the group meetings on the third floor he would tell us how his heroes fought for the utopian ideal, while we, the rejected wealthy nodded and waited for another smoke to pass us.

Eddie, who with his dreams and inability to fulfil them, found his calling in joining an imagined war across the river Thames. It was he, who along with an army of disgruntled anarchists attacked the Print barons in Wapping. On his soap box he suggested to us and quoting from the Socialist Worker, told us that, 'It was the current government that had taken the Times and its sister paper the Sun and relocated them to a cheaper electronic home in order to break the unions'. He wasn't a member himself, but the validity of the union was never questioned. We followed him to Wapping some evenings, out of nothing more than the curiosity to observe the historic battles. Bloodied idealists hurled bricks at the police and passing trucks and then walked back eating chips wrapped in the papers that were being targeted.

To the left of my flat was the home of the lost Punks, barely children, they were unwilling to return to their homes living in the fashion of Nihilism. They lost their right to electricity growing grubbier as the weeks past, until a police raid reunited them with the Social Services and their irate parents. When they left, we broke in to find they had been living on a diet of chocolate and were injecting powdered 'Lemsip' in the belief that it was amphetamines.

The last wire belonged to my friend. He was an illusive creature. A Scott by birth although weaned in the south. Hidden to the sunlight, he preferred to remain inside the curtained living quarters, neither, needing warmth or light. I would only be allowed into his home on occasions for he played music, sweet melodies that he wrote with poetry drawn from his darkness. I would accompany and he voiced the thoughts in the gloom. The words to his songs, he chalked on the plain walls, a crude but effective diary to those nights, charting the days that became his countdown. Today is four days away from the anniversary of his death.

Oxymoron

I swam skirting the shallows and tearing from shards of coral, speckled blood from my limbs causing clouds of sand and fluids to settle on the floor. She wanted me to do this and I wanted to do this for her to become one. She had not met my like before and I wanted her to be amazed at who I was splash . . . . foam. I am in her world. Only into air can we surface truly as one and only with clean fresh air can I draw breath. I have learned how to breathe the dank, dark, closed air from the shallows and it is where she and her like can be reached . . . paddle. Plink, splash. She can see me too, if she looks. Through my single glass lens, I spy the wet bronzed sucker lings, drying on the rocks I separate the shells with a sharp blade and hold their living forms and detach them from the rocks, as a lure to my world. When I find her she will be concealed but I shall find her for my determination is to be entwined in her arms. You too can reach out and touch her and look into her beautiful eyes so sharp, dedicated to catch her prey. Go on then. Go on camera capture her. Take her soul for my pleasure.

So I reach out and for a second become a green octopus in the sea of salt and she becomes my true 'Octimate.'

Guernsey Xmas Eve

It was the night that I lost my favourite amplifier lead. I have never been able to replace that particular cable and it has always been a reminder to me of that night, whenever I still play music professionally that my instrument is incomplete.

That particular night was the 24th of December, an eve of the yuletide and another booking for 'The worst Show on Earth,' a local folk band that lived up to its name. We were a five, six or whoever turned up, a folk tribute to the Dubliners and played through, rather than alongside the traditional Irish music scene for purely financial gain. Surprisingly we were popular on the Island, appealing to the many disposed population who looked across the water to the greener home without ever wishing to actually go back there. I too was a migrant worker and had landed many months before with a reason to escape the mainland. My hunger for greener pastures, were not for just money driven, the island gave me a chance to heal away from my personal demons in the solitude of the coastline. That night our music played and we drank a little between tunes. Our audience were that night predominantly Latvian all herb pickers who danced and ate from a bowl of crinkly cut chips, dowsed in vinegar and the sweet syrup of mayonnaise, as if it was the only hot meal that had eaten since leaving Riga months before. The music and the soulful Latvian eyes affected my playing that night. I watched the girls, for all were women, dreaming of the lovers they had left for a six-month working holiday. Each had a husband back home, as it was part of their visa that they were already married. The authorities when they arrived they display their married status, lest they mix with the locals and want to stay on the Island. They missed the music from their home and adopted us, and our music as a poor copy of their own traditional tunes. We reminded them of home and our live entertainment was welcomed. Like another migrant worker, we were all sailing on the boat that was this Island and without families of our own for this Christmas. At the end of the show I packed up my violin and collected my fee. The lead that I cherished was mixed in with the many other wires that were coiled, but I was too taken with a girl whose eyes had chanced on mine, to notice the loss. She spoke no English and I spoke no Latvian, but we agreed to be lovers and outside in the cold air kissed and thought of the people we had left at home. She left me in the car park, to return to her compatriots and I pulled up the collar of my coat around my cheeks holding the warmth that she had given me with her lips. I ferried myself around on an old motorcycle in those months, as it was cheap and as reckless as my behaviour. The violin was perched on my shoulder and I put on the crash hat to isolate the night. Sounds of revelling and mixed languages vanished into the vacuum of the protective headgear. Gloved, booted and suited in plastic trousers that I did not wish to show the new Latvian lover, I was ready to leave. The motorcycle was the cheapest vehicle I could have purchased and had treated me well, considering the abuse that I had shown it over the past year. Back home I had left my car, house a family, all were forgotten. My only priority when I left my home had been to rid myself, of the fear and shame of my recent breakdown. It was to this Island that I escaped and only occasionally did I think of others who had once depended on me. I had covered thousands of miles in the months away from the mainland and I had been away from home and it never once been let down mechanically. The motorcycle, a few clothes and the violin were all I allowed myself and were carried home that night from the gig. The violin had a belt attached to the strong case and its precarious balance was equalled by the lack of adhesion that motorcycle made to the road. I left the car park. The Latvians girls were still partying and would do so with their imported vodka when they returned to the tawdry house that they shared nearby. I was happy to leave them, as I had to be at a day job the next morning and was tired. She, the Latvian princess, left me her phone number, tattooed in biro to my wrist and promised me another night and another kiss.

The streets were deserted. It was not the night of the year when people were out in the streets. Either they were at home or in the midnight church services that kept the chapel lights burning. This left the streets empty and my path home uneventful. I lived on the side of the Island hedged by forestry and sheer drops. The district was called 'St. Martins,' it held the views of Normandy and a few exclusive properties, nestled in the shadow of the airport and a limited amount of cheap boarding houses. The airport was where small and medium sized aircraft landed throughout the day bringing people and news from the outside to the Island and its constant drone, for me was a comforting pleasure.

The gig that night was in a bar in the Northern end of the Island at St Sampson, another saint but a less successful one, for this end of the Island held the production and waste that gave most of the Island its industrial identity. The petroleum tanks jostled with a quaint harbour, but the gift shops did not venture here. I drove through unimpeded and covered the diagonal distance by a selection of tributary lanes through the un-signposted darkness. Chilled spittle's of cold air, pockets of ice grew between the warm housing that dotted the eight square miles of the Island accompanied the motorcycle and I. As I approached the junction between St Sampson's and De Mont, I hit a sheet of frozen tarmac, specially laid by Nature to deposit its Christmas greetings on the lone motorcyclist. There I began to freefall. Where I went or for how long in which direction mattered little. I stopped eventually without impacting on anything or anyone, and for that I am grateful. The violin, the cycle and rider were momentarily separated, brought back together and then discarded on different sides of the roadway. When we three stopped moving, my first instinct was to switch off the engine and get my violin off the carriageway, before someone passed by into its path. I picked up the cycle and put it on its stand then opened the violin case, took out the instrument and the bow. Tightening the horsehair, I played the first few bars of 'Oh come all ye faithful', just to prove that it had not lost the ability to sing and I had not my sense of humour.

In the distance the clock struck midnight and I welcomed in the season.

My motorcycle was less fortunate than the violin. A lever that attached to a delicate linkage had sheered off and stopped it from going into any gear, other than fourth. With another three miles ahead of me, I replaced my violin and set about the long walk back to my rooming house and sang to the night in full voice, my frosty breath globally warming the little Island I called home.

Birth and Death

The child was delivered blue/grey, a seal skin decaying gently in the protection of the womb. The mother has been induced and now lay asleep and unaware. He knew of the death and while she slept, he faced the sham of the birth. The birth had little joy, the pain was as great and then she was sedated. The reward of instant love was lost in the silence.

He stood at the edge of the bench and watched death enter this world in green overalls and white Wellingtons, the standard issue uniform to all in the operating theatre. Stopping the cross-infection to him seemed an unnecessary, given the diagnosis. In the mass of green and stainless steel someone spoke directly at him through their own mask.

'Do you want to hold her?"

He looked to the table and then at the nurse who was cutting the chord and parcelling up the child. He looked at his wife, she breathed calmly in her induced state of sleep.

'Do you want to touch her?' repeated the nurse

'You can hold her, if you think it will help.'

He shook his head, inside his mask; he kept the crooked line of his face, still knowing that if his lips parted they would release the cry his daughter should have made. Afterwards, he returned home and had the space to himself. The small terraced house in Dumfries was to have been the welcome to a third person and now he was alone. His wife slept for hours after the birth and when she woke he told her the truth. She had suspected that something was wrong when it stopped moving inside her. Her reaction was cold and she asked to hold the child, brushing the baby's face as if it would react to her touch. Then she let go and sank back into her pillows while the young nurse took the body away. He left her to the professionals and now had to make the round of phone calls to announce the death. He could not talk to anyone and began clearing the toys, clothes, and preparation of the child that should be there with them. Taking the items that they had purchased for the baby he opened the under stair cupboard. The darkness welcomed him so he left the baby's toys outside and climbed into the void and closed the door on the evil of the world. There he travelled back to his past life in Northern Island.

In the dugout he would be safe. Lined with heather and protected from the night he sat four foot beneath the roots of an oak in the no mans land.

The County of Ballymena lies adjoining the Eire border. It is a place where many illicit deals and events take place. Being that the Republicans' do not believe that a border should even exist, this imaginary line does not instil any reverence to some and to the authorities it is a convenient line on their maps, which has to be patrolled. He is sunken into the ground as he can observe without detection. The darkness stops time for him. He watches blackness counting his breaths, in the unseen warmth thinks about returning to his wife for the paternity leave he will soon have.

Waking to the Morning after

It is the morning, or is this evening? I am awake, but I should be sleeping. A tongue lined with carpet, ears that are sandwiched between a slice of toast and a plate. My fingers are attached to someone else's feet, or are they? This is not a room that I know of, or a place I could recognise if I did. I fell from my dream; except that dreams are sober things and mine are not. Smells permeate into my eyes absorbed by the grease that drips from the carpet-flavoured mouth. In between my fingernails there are fish that swim in irregular patterns. How am I lying, and does it matter? At this angle I can walk on the ceiling in someone's slippers that I have stolen from the waste bin. My bloated nostrils cry for water to ease the spring that coils behind my eyes, unravelled the sinews of every pore seep from a loose memory from the grey matter as it leaves my body between my toes.

I want to tell, you need to hear, and we need to talk, unless I fear you are, like me, dead to the world. The flat earth on which I will lie across is waiting for me to vomit the history that was last night. Four feet pointed upward. Two hands clasped, not to each other. One memory, merged with another falsehood. Remind me. Never, never let me drink again.

The Park in '76

My cycle parked on its side stand. It's not any two-wheeled vehicle. It's a yellow and Chrome-clad 'Chopper'. Bee inspired paint, blue and white decals, red-rimmed tyres designed to increase the sense of speed. I'm a human harnessed engine, parker-hooded, baseball boots laces trailing dangerously to the ground, a weekend ahead of this ten year old. Our summer stretches ahead of the evaporating estate, youthful occupants wanting to discard their clothes, although too hot to wear, they are too fashionable to be without. Out from the safety of the shed, I sit astride and focus before pushing the silver pedals, sunlight colliding in the reflector as they spin, delivering me from the house to the swings. Our park is devoid of parental control and adult rules and I embrace the freedom. My parker coat is of sheer nylon thread. I did want a canvas 'Mod' Coat, because my friends own one, a uniform to allow me to join the others. I like the fur collar and the plunging pointed back. Even the padded interior of orange nylon appeals to me. I want to lift the hood away from my sweating face but cannot put it down, as my shirt is not smart enough to be seen.

At the swings we meet. Cycles clashing against cycle, spokes and clackers calling to each other as do their owners in our special language of the children. From different corners of the green, three school friends who have eaten their 'Ready break' breakfasts, meet at the swings. We have a day ahead while our parents work in the factory. A radio plays at the swings, Marc sings to us, and the older teens talk of his latest album, even though they do not own it.

Older than me, the boys and girls are learning to be together, they kiss and 'Shang-a-lang' to the next song from the transistor radio and I wish that I could age two years to join them. By growing into teens they have lost their desire to ride bicycles and swing in the fenced area until called back for tea. My brother, he is one of them, his face is pressed against Tracy Blessed's spotty mouth between drags of her number six filters. I am not allowed to acknowledge the brother with whom I share a room at night, my two years lessen my status, and I am not to break his rules.

John, my friend of two years arrives. We nod, and in that nod remember that we have pledged blood allegiance. I want to be like him, and I later learn he wants to be like me.

"You ready?" John says to me. His cycle is one of the five speed racing machines that we have all have wanted to purchase from 'Blacks' cycles.

"We could go to Streatham. 'Be back before tea," he says, setting the challenge.

We have made a pact, when one makes the game we have to follow.

"I can't be later than five," says Kelly. "It's a 'Vesta' night."

We all understand. I like the chow mien with the crispy noodles from the packet.

"I want to go," repeats John "if we go now, we could be back before tea."

We both know that this is not true. Kelly has a Raleigh with small wheels, and no gears, he will never keep up. Kelly knows what we are thinking, "Jo won't keep up on his Chopper." He says turning to me sinking his eyes into their sockets in distain. He does not want to go; he has never been further than the end of the next street. He pulls a wheelie and turns his bike back to face the safety his home.

"I still want to go." I tell John. I know John has made up his mind and will go alone if I let him, just to make a point.

"It'll mean crossing Crystal Palace," he says.

"I can do it." I reply.

We both look to Kelly who turns the handlebars and steers towards his corner of the park. "I'm going," he sneers and we ignore him.

John looks at me, his eyes mellow and he pulls at the collar of his patterned shirt across the sides of his cheek, trying to look bigger. It does not matter to him if I join him or not because John has a life of independence in front of him and I am a follower. Kelly is a small spec at the other side of the green and he is looking away from us. We are the explorers and we will have the story to tell.

"You won't need your coat," says John with some foresight, "it'll only slow you up on the hill."

John is right, John is always right.

My brother is still at the swings, his mouth still stuck to the spotty girl from our street. I break his rules and walk up to my older sibling. He looks at me through her face and I see his anger in his eyes. I take off my coat and offer it to him to keep it safe while I'm away. He separates the sucker and tells me to "Piss off." So I roll up my coat, taking out my conker and the house key, and shove it in between the broken slats of the roundabout for safekeeping. We turn to the gates and begin our journey. Selecting first, second and third, John changes further into his fourth and leaves me with his increased speed. We race towards the gated ironwork and aiming for the entrance and gathering the cold breeze into our chests as we rise over the exit to a world outside. Free from the park we cross the border, green following us, not us following the green. My trousers flap in time with the spinning spokes. John laughs at my heavy frame struggling and sees the bumps, depressing the sprung seat. He leaves me behind. I am out classed and John knows it.

Ahead of us are the grey pathways, pavements of tarmac that lead us across the whole world, should we choose to follow them. John slows to a stop by the main road. His brakes squeal as he thinks late when stopping. His centre pulled callipers calling anger to his halt. I draw up beside him. We watch the traffic pass through the main road. It is our first major obstacle.

"We could always go next week," he says ashamedly.

I know that he is a little afraid and was caught up in the moment. His reputation is at stake. But I will not judge him, as he is my best friend.

'Don't tell Kelly!' He asks of me.

I agree. It will be our secret linked by the blood between us. Of course we did go, but not that day. I cycle back to the swings, where I retrieve my coat. We are safe for another day.

A Bridge to Fear

While we are playing bridge, I wonder what would happen if the card that was turned up would be of value to my partner. Julia studies her hand. I study her hands, holding the cards and look up to her face. The sheen from the pack, reflects light, bouncing off the spades, hearts or clubs she holds. There are no diamonds. She does not have the right hand for I know that myself, or one of our opponents, holds them.

The opposition does not matter for they are, for this evening, our competitor's, not that this competition is of any real value, monetarily or momentarily. The couple who have joined us this evening have only answered our invitation because of Julia Sedgly, or Doctor Julia Sedgly, to give her true title, not that her position matters to the game, but her position matters. Her status is the bait we use to encourage the persons now sitting by our side. The Doctor always does have the social clout.

I pause in my thoughts and look at Julia in front of me at the green table. She winks, the cards are good. Our quick connection is made, the secret language of players who know a secret hand. The couple at either side of the table do not know our language, or our cards.

'I could do with a drink!' says Clive, the husband to my left, 'you want one Margery?'

Her pearls rattle as she nods. The tension of the game seemed to matter to this couple.

'What did you say you did?' asks Clive, for the second time as Julia pours water into two glasses from the pitcher on the table.

I did not answer for I cannot. They are uncomfortable and did not expect this social event would turn this way. Socially, this game is usually a way of breaking through society, this evening Clive and Margery hoped for an opportunity to develop their struggling business, little did they know that this was going to be our night.

'We were so looking forward to having you for dinner,' said Julia. When they spoke on the telephone Dr Julia Sedgly engaged our opponents with the promise of a game of bridge and potential introductions to our strata.

'Yes we do play', said Clive, 'Margery and I can certainly make up a rubber.'

Then he asked for the address and was hooked. Only on arrival did they shudder a little at the state of the house.

'She's a pathologist?' said Margery, 'you would think that they could afford better.'

The door opened, and the said Doctor welcomed our guests. Julia now slips her foot across to mine under the table; she is ready to place down her cards. Clive wants to drink from his glass but cannot reach the water; the boarded windows have not been mentioned. I am not a medic. My interest is in the aesthetic. Between us, Julia and I have opposite passions, she the science and I the image.

'There,' said Julia placing down her cards and smiling at me. We both look to our respective opposites to see their reaction.

'We win,' says Julia. The couple have little response, after all this is the third hour.

Clive has an eye on the door. He only has a hand free to hold the cards. The flex that holds him and his wife to their chairs restricts all other movement.

'Margery' Clive quietly says to his wife. 'We should really be going, don't you think?'

She has lost the power to speak. Julia gets up from the table and walks across to the window.

'George I think we need to turn in now. I'll just switch this off.' Julia walks across to the video camera and presses the off button.

'Darling do come over and see.'

I manoeuvre myself from the table, my batteries powering the chair across to the camera to witness the recorded event.

'Time to go,' says Julia, striding over to the green felted table and our guests.

'Thank you for your time, my husband and I have so little company these days.'

Clive watches horrified as, firstly Julia dispatches his wife and then turns to him with her scalpel and cuts him cleanly and professionally. The Doctor severs the bodies from the chairs ready to remove the parts I require. I patiently wait, wondering what would happen next. Minutes pass by, turning into hours and then a familiar voice resonates and I know instinctively that everything will be all right.

Case History of 'J'

She, for it is a she who watches the doorway and has without question, had enough. The doorway has been opened, just enough to pass a beaker full on entry and empty on its return. A green juice mixture is sent by one of her carer's on the hour and when drunk, returned back to the waiting hand. Although the doorway is open, there is no light no ultra-violet is allowed to pass through the sealed house. Heavy drapes hold off the creep of the morning, prolonging and Forever night, which suits her. She has a room and that room is hers, the whole house is hers, yet for the past three years, she has not found it safe or needed to leave the one cell, a cell she has made for herself. Every action takes place within this space; her toilet, sleep of which there is very little and breath are all taken within 12 X 12 feet of plaster. Darkness is her necessity; she has chosen the darkness, as it is neutral and being neutral is comforting, so it says on her file. The file is updated with each visit yet reads the same from its initial page to the present.

'This is her file, this is her pen and I am her keeper and have been for three years'.

'What are you saying?'

I might have said the bit about the file out loud and she has heard me, I have broken the vow of silence, the rule to speak only when addressed. She does not like me to make a sound, sound together with light and water, are her greatest fears. She has a name but I cannot as a professional mention it to anybody. We have a job to do and part of that job does not go beyond these walls. It is the part of our credibility to be discreet, that and to be honest, which for me has never been in question, or proved. There are writings in the file that are confidential, even to the client and she is our paymaster. The medical authorities are aware that too much information could be a dangerous additive to the present crisis. I thought that we were just not allowed to gossip but as with any rule in social work speak, there is a long fangled word that means the same thing and we have to follow this protocol. Confidentiality is so overrated.

'Drink!' she calls me occasionally to request. A single word usually tires her and sometimes it is just a grunt, which at that part of the day I can relate to her routine and needs. Whether, it is to drink the boiled green tea, micro-waved to ten seconds, stopped at eight seconds on the dial so the ping does not upset her or the further covering of some miscreant light source that has broken into her space. She can open the door for a few seconds to pass out her toilet remains. Our hands never touch for the contact would probably kill her, or so she says. She calls me the name of the last carer, when I know that I am John. I stay here for 25 hours a week. There are eleven of us regularly visiting, so you can appreciate the chances of always having a female in post are difficult for the agency. She has never actually seen me and I have been instructed by the outside world to keep my voice as light as possible. She has read the sound of my breathing as female, for which she has assigned a name. She has and never will actually see me although I can always see her. He face is etched into my memory as she stands here and in the once pleasant photograph of her that sits in a plastic sleeve in her file.

'Drink!!!'

There she is again. I put the cup into the white machine outside her door and set the timer. Sometimes it is worth the trouble she will give me, to let the ping happen. It is cruel but she deserves to be reminded of our control sometime. This drink is her only form of nutrition and is made by a local herbalist. She believes in his un-educated guessing and potions. She has fought the social services over his methods and her use of him. She is paying for these expenses, so they relented to keep her behaviours stable. She has a phobic reaction to contact with her skin of water-based cleansers and this has developed into a fear of water penetrating to her insides. Water scalds her, so she says and it is as if she has trained her skin to redden at the thought of being washed. The green mush she ingests is not water, that's what she thinks. She has told her carers that it is a fruit based alcohol that can supplement her need for water. We know this to be a falsehood for we mix the green syrup with tap water before we heat it up for her. No one dares to tell her and she has not noticed yet. She drinks this stuff, gurgling supping it gently. We never actually see her drink, but the beaker always returns empty. The beaker has chew marks on the edge, which shows us that her teeth are still functioning. She insists on this cup as anything else can pick up germs. She cleans it herself with the same baby wipes that she uses to wash her body.

'Drink done',

I have never been into her room. I sometimes think that this is just a game she is playing to test the system, pretending to be ill, having all of us running around her while she festers in her own filth behind the door. The truth could be that behind the door she is living a full and rewarding life with communications, washing from glacial waters piped in from the outside and laughing at us who are made to serve her. I would love her to have one second of normality with a few of the pleasures society expects us to enjoy, but she seemingly wants none of it. This is how I now that she is ill, sick of living and unable to change it. The truth about real sickness is that the person who lives within it has no choice. She is sick because no one would want to live like that.

Magic at home

'I place the miniature doll's chair down on the table like so. Place the silk handkerchief over the chair.' We watched as Uncle Victor the Magician did exactly that.

'And now we whisper the magic words,' this no one understood which was fortunate considering what occurred next. Uncle Victor's moustache twitched with gleeful playfulness and the edges of his mouth-curled outwards. He knew this trick and had used it many times when his act was flagging. This is where I have been instructed to turn out the light. On cue, I flick the switch, releasing the light from its power source. There is blackness and before the group of twenty young cynics have adjusted to the blackness, Uncle Victor has changed.

'On', he commands and I scrabble for the plastic button, depressing it with urgency and sending a shaft of energy back to the cooling bulb.

Uncle Victor has vaporized. Not just left the room, for there is an incandescent glow around the space that he once was. Above the silken rag and the small doll's chair a trail of smoke hangs deceptively over the tabletop. Then beneath the silk handkerchief a rustling begins, like two mice fighting over a lump of cheese followed by the reduced figure of Uncle Victor sitting on the doll's chair, perfectly miniature and measuring four inches high.

Uncle Victor jumps up from his chair; a little squeaky voice from the table shouts 'Tara!' disbelief at the illusion before them.

The magician, who has transformed himself before them, raises his arms and then triumphantly and then returns to his seat before turning to me and shouts in falsetto.

'All right Charles you can switch the light off again.'

I once again flick the switch and the room is again in darkness, except for wails of the children there is no other noticeable distraction and after counting the prescribed six seconds I again return the room to light.

Uncle Victor is once again full size and standing before the children.

The silk handkerchief is returned to his pocket and the doll's chair in his outstretched palm.

'That foxed 'em', said Uncle Victor turning to me. Below us the howls of the audience were once again naive children at a birthday party.

'They'll think again before telling me that I'm not a real magician!' he said with, what I thought was a spiteful edge to his voice.

We left ten minutes later, without our fee as Mrs Sanderson; the Birthday boy's mother said that she had booked a conjurer and not a witch. Uncle Victor did not take this as an insult and was content to leave having miniaturized the family silver for his later use, which he assured me would make more at auction than our fee.

Letter to Martha

Oh Martha, I went out last week and noticed how underdressed I was compared to Harvey. You know Harvey, he is that young man whom Jessica had been seeing until last Fall after that time she had that business with her, well lets say it was an indiscretion she could not handle. So Harvey and I were out together, Thursday I believe it must have been, because on Wednesday I was chasing around town with Charles and his friends. Oh Charles, let me tell you has a new girl, won't tell me who, or even if it is a girl. Says the name is Frank and age twenty-three, by his usual form that is dog years, oh must not mock my little brother. But then he has past much meat to my plate. Harvey, Harvey, Harvey, what a lovely name. Apparently it is the surname of the man who discovered that blood pumps the blood around the body. Well this Harvey got my pulse racing! Thursday, there I was sitting down in a punt while he plunged his long pole into the watery mire of the river. I looked up at him and saw through the foliage of the hanging willow, a colossus of a man with starbursts around his head. If I weren't already reclining then I would have swooned there and then.

Harvey is, had, wants to start, something to do in business. He had an Austin, not one of those you sees everyday, and he says that it is customized by a little workshop, or maybe that is his business. I forget, anyway he is such a good listener; I am surprised that Jessica let him down so badly, considering how much she has to say about herself. We all managed all of these bridges before he took off his tie. Eton I think he said it was or maybe I just wish it was an Eton tie. Charles was at Eton, for a while. Do you remember Terrance? He was at Eton. I had such a thing for him too. He took me to a school ball and I got a little squiffy beforehand and then was sick in the Rhododendrons or was it the Clematis? Must remember to ask Janet, she was with us that do you remember? Well Harvey took off his tie and then his shirt and then his pumps. I was intrigued to see the man under the costume, you can tell so much about a man without his socks. So mummy says. I do miss Mummy, it is the 2nd anniversary since, since she left Daddy and me and went off to Cloisters with the tennis coach from the club. He didn't even ski. What was she thinking of. She always said she could tell a thing about socks. Why was I talking of socks? Oh Harvey. Well he had biceps they were curved so perfectly that I found myself looking at his arms and the light bouncing off them as he handled the boat so manfully.

If I had known that Jessica and Harvey were going together officially I would never have of stepped on her toes. Harvey was there in his socks and it seemed only right that I loosen my straps and then it just happened. He wasn't looking where we were going, hit the bank and over he went. Splash! It was only a small bump that made him topple in. I think it was that reminded me that he was supposed to land elsewhere, on Jessica most probably.

Well when he finally surfaced, I was fully dressed and looking to an easy disembarkation. He might have lovely arms but he had promised me lunch and there was no way I was going to be seen with him in that condition. B x

Tree of Love

In the tree's canopy, suspended by branches, green arms of foliage, legs dangle down, arms balanced, the bodies high above the ground floor brush, sleeping. Heat rising, push a cushion of air against the gentle undulations of breath. Dream's of excitement, twitching the extensions of their limbs in accordance with the winds. Two are held, balanced in a dance of love. One wakes to return to the real world. A tap to the others bare shoulder gently calls. Do not tap too furiously lest either of you plummet to the grasses beneath.

She and he have climbed up to the top most branches, entwined in the greenery after excusing themselves from the others. Away from many disapproving eyes their friends play, drinking in the fresh air of the countryside. Hidden above they have climbed away from prying eyes they journeyed to where the world sways ship like, wafting on a sea of green. Hidden in these heights, they touch each other, undressing and exploring each other at the topmast of the tree, away from the gaze of the Churchmen, elders below directing the non-secular picnic. Two of Gods own children, inquisitive and naked, fumble their clothing draped across twigs, making love as do the birds until, chilled and lost they find a branch and spread out their spent carcasses to sleep and sun. Here they sleep and grow tanned until after an hour of sleep and the game below is finished, the Reverend adorns his robes and affixes his glasses to his face, calls his flock to pack for the journey home. He begins to count the children. All God's children are present.

'To the bus' he commands, they sheep like fall into line and wandering together to the coach parked in the car park. The missing two dress, kiss each other perhaps for the last time and descend to join the others below.

'Are, there you are,' spouts the vicar, 'missed a good game of Rounders.'

There is no explanation from the two Sunday school teachers. If only the minister had looked up he would have seen the devil at play. On the bus home they all sing.

'All things bright and beautiful all creatures great and small, the Lord God made them all.'